She Was Mine First

USA TODAY & WALL STREET JOURNAL BESTSELLING AUTHOR

M. ROBINSON

SHE WAS MINE FIRST

M. ROBINSON

© 2023 She Was Mine First by M. Robinson

All rights Reserved.
No part of this book may be used or reproduced in any manner whatsoever without written permission of the author.
This book is a work of fiction. References to real people, events, establishments, organizations, or locations are intended only to provide a sense of authenticity and are used fictitiously. All characters are a figment of the author's imagination, and all incidents and dialogue are drawn from the author's mind's eye and are not to be interpreted as real. Though several people, places, and events portrayed in this book are correct, the story is fiction that the author has made up for entertainment purposes only.

To all the readers who love their friends to lovers romances with lots of angst and heat that leaves a mark.

I wrote this for you.

Prologue
ETHAN

Have you ever had a connection with someone so fucking deep you can feel them from across the world?

It was where time and distance knew no bounds, and it almost seemed as if the further you were away from one another, the closer you'd feel to each other.

From my mind to my body to my soul...

Livvy Collins had always owned every last part of me.

We'd been best friends since we were kids. I couldn't remember a time when she wasn't the most important person in my life. I couldn't remember a memory that didn't involve her in some way, shape, or form. The list of things I couldn't forget about her was endless.

From her laughter to her smile to her intoxicating scent... taste... feel...

It didn't matter what life put us through, our friendship always came first. From friends to lovers to friends again, our unbreakable bond remained the same—even after we fell in love with each other.

Separate colleges.

Multiple relationships.

Different careers.

Not one milestone changed anything between us. If anything, our friendship became stronger despite the odds of it. Through it all, we were always there for one another.

And that night at three in the morning was no fucking exception.

I felt her before I ever heard my cell ring. Shooting straight up in my hotel suite bed, I woke up from a dead sleep seconds before my phone actually rang. Not thinking twice about it, I didn't have to check the screen to know it was her.

Instead, I answered, "Are you okay?"

She giggled. "Is that any way to answer your phone?"

I sighed in relief. "It is when you call me at this time of night."

"Well... I'm surprised you're not working."

"Who says I'm not?"

"I can hear it in your tone," she playfully informed. "You were sleeping."

"Livvy, even when I'm sleeping, you know I'm still working."

"I guess the more things change, the more they stay the same, huh?"

"Are you calling to ride my ass about working too much?"

"I would never," she mocked in a condescending tone that made me grin.

"Just think of how much the Beauet stock would collapse if your app wasn't number one?"

"So you did call to ride my ass."

She giggled again. "Is Celeste with you?"

"Celeste and I aren't together anymore."

"You were together two nights ago."

"That was two nights ago."

"Another one bites the dust, I see?"

"Livvy, you know I don't have time for that."

"You have time for me."

"I make time for you," I stressed, lying back on the bed. "There's a difference."

I didn't have to see her face to know she was smiling on the other end of the phone.

"I'm going to hold you to that."

"What's this about?" My eyebrows pinched together as she hesitated for a second.

"Where are you?" she asked, sounding so far away.

"In a hotel suite in Canada."

"Far from home then."

Narrowing my eyes, I repeated her question. "Where are you?"

"On the balcony of an estate in Colorado."

"Livvy, what—"

"I need you, Ethan."

I immediately asked, "What's with all the cryptic? Are you alright?"

"I've never been better." She paused for a moment, and I could sense her hesitation.

"You think you can take time off from work for the next week?"

"Not until you tell me why?" I cautiously waited for I don't know what.

"I just need my best friend."

I abruptly sat up, about to respond, but she would have knocked me on my ass if I wasn't already sitting down. It all happened so fast, yet it still seemed as if it played out in slow motion.

She unexpectedly revealed, "I'm getting married."

"What—"

She cut me off, bluntly adding...

"And I need you to be my man of honor."

Chapter One
LIVVY

THE BEGINNING: FOURTEEN YEARS OLD

I spent the entire summer riding my bike with my best friend Ethan Carter. We met on the school bus halfway through first grade. I was the new kid in his town and school, and he shared his seat with me on the bus so I didn't have to sit alone. From that moment forward, we were inseparable.

My dad got a huge promotion at work, and that was why we had to move to Charleston, South Carolina. It seemed like it happened overnight. He became the vice president of some big company, and all I knew was that he was an important person.

Our small town knew who my father was, and he never let me forget it. Don't get me wrong, he was a great dad and I loved him very much, but appearances were his top priority. He constantly reminded me that my bad decisions would reflect on our family, and I took that advice seriously.

Ethan's life was very different from mine. He lived a few blocks from my house, outside the gates of the private community where I lived. His mom passed away from cancer when he was a baby, so he didn't remember her at all. His father didn't handle her death well, and Ethan's uncle adopted him instead. He moved in with his mom's brother before he started preschool. So his uncle was raising him and worked a lot.

Despite how often I asked Ethan over the years, he never spoke about his father. Since his uncle was not part of my father's elite country club or an important figure in our town, my dad wasn't fond of our friendship.

However, this was where my mom came through for me. She stepped in to remind Dad that this was my life, and I could choose who I wanted to be friends with as long as they weren't a bad influence, which was the only reason my father didn't object. Ethan's family wasn't on the same status as mine, but he was wicked smart. His grades and academic achievements were in the top 10 percent of our middle school, and everyone knew who he was.

Teachers.

Principals.

Parents.

They all wanted their kids to use him as an example. My mom always had my back when it came to our friendship. I think what bothered my father the most was that Ethan was a boy instead of girl best friend like most girls my age had.

Thank God he worked around the clock, so I never really worried about him running into Ethan in our house, but even when they did cross paths, my mom was the housewife and caretaker at the end of the day. My father might make the rules, but she enforced them, and lucky for me, she liked Ethan a lot.

"Come on, Livvy!" Ethan shouted. "You're dragging your feet!"

"I'm just trying not to break my neck on this dumb skateboard!"

"Stop being so dramatic and kick your foot faster like I taught you!"

It didn't matter how fast I kicked my foot. I'd never be able to catch up to him. My legs were much shorter than his, and he knew it too. Ethan was baiting me. It was one of his favorite things to do, along with endlessly teasing me.

I yelled back out of breath, "I am kicking my foot, Ethan!"

"Stop being a girl and kick your foot faster!"

"Ugh!"

By the time I caught up to him, it was only because he stopped at the end of the street to wait for me. This was Ethan to a T. One minute, he was picking on me. The next, he was handing me a ladybug that he always seemed to find for me. They meant love and good luck, and he knew how much I loved them.

I smiled. "How do you always find them?"

"What can I say?" He grinned. "The ladies love me."

I rolled my eyes, scoffing out a chuckle. "Humble much?"

"I'm just stating facts."

He wasn't lying. Girls had been flocking to my best friend ever since I could remember. They never mattered, though. Ethan didn't show any interest in their attention. He wasn't like normal fourteen-year-old boys obsessed with boobs and getting to second base.

Despite being popular and having friends who were exactly that, Ethan was quiet.

Reserved.

Kind of broody.

Very serious.

Especially when we were around other people.

He could always read them for what they were, and he didn't let anyone see the sides of him that he openly showed me when we were alone. I loved having him to myself when I didn't have to share him with anyone. I never thought anything of it.

What girl wants to share her best friend?

I thought the feelings I had for him were normal.

"I'm going to punch you," I playfully sassed.

He smiled, handing me the ladybug. "Yeah... well it wouldn't hurt even if you did."

Before I could jokingly hit him, he took off on his skateboard. Ethan was a much better skater than I was, but there weren't many things that he wasn't good at. Our teachers called him gifted.

After what seemed like forever, we reached the waterhole in the woods. Ethan found this place a few years ago, and it sort of became our secret spot. Nobody knew about it but us.

This was the place where lines were crossed, boundaries were blurred, and limits were tested. The tightrope of our friendship would eventually snap in our faces without us ever expecting it for one second.

I slid off my shirt and shorts, throwing them onto a tree branch by the grass. Wearing a purple one-piece bathing suit, I made my way to the water when I heard Ethan haul ass from behind me, jumping headfirst into the river. As soon as he appeared from under the water, he whipped his hair back away from his face and swam closer to the bank, waiting for me.

I scrunched my face and tottered through the swampy grass, my feet sinking to the bottom of my slippery steps. Ethan jerked his head to the side, causing me to smirk. It was our silent agreement for me to hang off his back. I smiled and swam up behind him, putting my arms around his neck and my legs around his torso.

I watched him swing off the rope into the water for the next hour. He had tied it to a tree last month, but I had yet to do it.

"Your turn," he coaxed, swimming up beside me.

"Ummm... no, I'm good."

I wasn't the best swimmer, and the current could change, easily dragging me along.

As if reading my mind, he reminded me, "You know I'd never let anything happen to you."

"You can't control the river's current, Ethan."

He cocked his head to the side. "I can control you, though."

I arched an eyebrow, waiting...

For what, I don't know.

ETHAN

A part of me always knew she was aware of the emotions she stirred inside me. It didn't matter what she was doing. My eyes followed her everywhere, constantly waiting for her to do something else to make me fall in love with her a little more.

I thought it was normal...

The feelings I had for her. I learned later that I was wrong. I couldn't have been more wrong if I tried. Livvy's and my friendship was never complicated until it was. I guess that was what happened when you meet your soulmate as a kid and instantly become best friends.

We should have known.

It would have saved us from years of mistakes and time lost of us being together that way.

"You weigh eighty pounds wet, Livvy."

I was the only person to call her that. Everyone else called her Liv or Elizabeth.

Livvy was only my nickname for her.

"If the current shifts," I added with a smile. "I can control you from being dragged with it."

"Yeah? Well, I don't want to test that theory."

"All right," I snapped, hitting my breaking point of her fear not letting her enjoy this with me. "I've had enough of this." With that, I caught her by the waist right before she was about to haul ass and run away. Throwing her over my shoulder, I carried her to the rope.

"No, no, no, no, no," she repeated, kicking her legs and squirming her body around.

"We're going to do it together," I demanded. "Stop fighting me, Livvy. I'll put you right on my back, and all you have to do is hang on."

She sighed deeply, quickly giving in. She could never say no to me.

"Fine, but you have to promise that you won't let go of me once we hit the water."

In a sincere tone, I swore, "I promise."

Chapter Two

ETHAN

In one swift movement, I shifted her body to my back. "Now hang on, and whatever you do, don't let go of me," I ordered.

She took another deep breath and nodded. I grabbed the rope, looking back at her for a second before she squeezed her eyes shut and bit her bottom lip.

"Don't bite your lip. You ready?"

She hesitated. "Nooo…"

"I'll jump on the count of three—one, two, three," I exclaimed, pushing our bodies into the air as she locked her ankles around my stomach and squeezed the shit out of my neck with her arms.

We hit the river in a hard splash, causing her to release me instantly. I paddled up to the surface as fast as I could, but I was too late. My heart lodged itself in my throat as I looked all around me. My adrenaline kicked into overdrive, replacing all my emotions except for the urgency to find her. Until finally, I did. I didn't have time to catch my breath before I was kicking my feet in her direction.

Her head was suddenly above water as she coughed, "Ethan! Help!"

A few feet in front of me, she was towed by the strong current.

I immediately felt horrible, pissed at myself for not listening to her in the first place. Trying to shake off the guilt, I swam faster to her.

Hurrying over, I grabbed her foot while the current continued to drag her, and I didn't falter for one second, yanking her toward me with such force that it knocked me back too.

She started to panic, trying to climb me to keep her head above water.

"Livvy." I spit out water, holding us both up. "Relax, or you'll drown us both."

She did, and I was able to flip her over onto her back to keep her face up so she could breathe as I pulled her toward the bank. I didn't expect the current to feel this strong as I towed her body to where she could step. The stream felt completely different when I swam alone.

"Livvy, kick your feet!" I shouted.

Once she started to, I was able to get us to the shoreline much faster and easier. I was still out of breath by the time I felt the ground beneath me. Livvy stepped down shortly after I did, and we locked eyes. Both of us panted as our chests heaved and our stares widened. I could see the tears forming in her eyes, only making me feel worse.

Livvy didn't cry.

Ever.

"I told you!" she yelled, immediately ripping into me. "I told you I didn't want to go out there! Why would you do that to me?"

"Livvy, calm down," I reasoned, grabbing her arms to help her in. Tugging her toward me, I held her tighter against me. "You're okay. I'm so sorry, but you're okay."

She thrashed in my arms. "Ethan Carter, let go of me!"

"Don't be like this."

"Don't be like what? I could have drowned!"

"You were never going to drown."

"How do you know? You think you know everything!"

"Livvy…"

"Don't Livvy me in that tone! Now let go!"

"No," I argued. "Not until you forgive me."

She screamed, drawing back far enough that I had to grip her wrists.

"Stop screaming," I ordered, shaking my head.

"Then let go of me!" she countered through gritted teeth near my face.

"Are you going to forgive me?" I asked, not backing down.

"Absolutely not."

"You're such a stubborn little thing." I jerked her forward, closer to my face and she lost her footing.

She wouldn't stop fighting while I just held on to her, barely breaking a sweat or using any of my strength. She knew her efforts wouldn't matter. She would never be able to overpower me and get away. I was bigger, and she wasn't going anywhere unless I wanted her to. I knew that pissed her off more than anything.

"Stop being such a girl," I simply stated.

Her eyes widened, loudly gasping. "Oh my God! Let go! Let go of me right now!"

"Fine!" I released her, and she stumbled back, glaring right at me. I'd never seen her so mad.

"You're an asshole!"

"Enough with the attitude. I'm sorry, but there's no way I'd ever let anything happen to you, and you know that."

And then she pushed me, like full-on shoved me, and I barely wavered, which only infuriated her to push me again. My eyes widened, surprised and partly amused with her feisty spirit that always did things to me.

I did the only thing I could think of. Acting on pure impulse, I tackled her to the soft grass. Laying my body on top of hers, I held her in place beneath me.

"Do you need a hug? Is that what this is about?" I teased in a high-pitched voice, holding her tighter.

"Oh my God, Ethan! This is cheating!"

I didn't hesitate, reaching down to grip her inner thigh, and she immediately lost her shit. Laughing and thrashing all around, she whipped her body, trying to break free from my relentless torture.

"See..." I smiled. "All you needed was some of my love."

We'd been saying we loved each other for as long as I could remember. Again, I thought it was normal. You're supposed to love your best friend regardless of them being a girl.

"Are you done now?" I tickled her other thigh.

"Stop!" She laughed out, trying to catch her breath.

"Say the magic words, and I will."

"I hate you!" She laughed harder.

"Now you're going to have to apologize too."

"You're horrible!"

"And you love me for it."

"Ethan, you're shameless!"

"Say you're sorry, and you didn't mean it!"

"Never!"

"Then I'm not going to stop until you do."

"Please!" she begged, at her wit's end.

"Say you forgive me."

She screamed, falling into a fit of giggles. "Okay! I forgive you, and I didn't mean it."

Unable to stop, I added, "Now tell me you love me."

"Ugh!" She wiggled some more. "I love you!"

I finally halted my attack, sitting back on my knees, and she took the momentum of my movement to push me, making me fall into the grass.

"Jerk!" She stood, smiling down at me with a satisfied expression on her face.

"You'll pay for that." I grinned.

She rolled her eyes, reaching her hand down to help me up. It took me a few seconds to trust her not to shove me back into the grass again. I could see it in her smug smirk that she was going to. Before she could, I grabbed her hand and yanked her down on top of me instead. She fell onto my chest, and we both began laughing.

It was only then we realized how close our mouths were to one another. Neither one of us had ever been this close to anyone's lips before. Hers parted, sucking in a breath. This was the first time I felt something drastically change between us, but before I could give it any more thought, she blinked, and the fire in her stare was gone.

"Only you would make me fall with you! You're such a bully sometimes!" She pushed off my chest to back away. "I can't believe you—"

Using her own momentum, I gripped the back of her neck and tugged her toward me, right onto my lips. A million thoughts ran through my head, but the second I felt her mouth on mine, they were all gone. Nothing else mattered at that moment.

I had no idea what I was doing. My heart sped so fast that I swear she could hear it. It was the most overwhelming feeling I'd ever had.

My lips started to open, and she followed my lead, parting hers in the same rhythm as mine. Our mouths moved in sync with each other, like we'd been kissing all of our lives.

At least it felt that way for me.

My tongue touched her lips, and it was the craziest sensation as I pulled back my tongue so she could softly slide hers into my mouth. I tasted what was left of her honey lip gloss, knowing I'd never be able to smell that scent and not think of her.

I pecked her lips one last time and gently pulled away from her, leaving her breathless. Our eyes slowly opened at the same time, and I saw something in hers I'd never seen before.

Her pupils were dilated, and the emerald-green pools that I was so used to were gone. The two big black rings I saw held so much emotion that it was almost overpowering, yet I didn't know what that meant. It scared me not to recognize my best friend, but at the same time, it was just as exciting.

I let her go, and she lightly touched her lips, swiping her fingers back and forth on her mouth. I watched her every move with an intense glare that had me trying to understand what had just happened between us.

I couldn't move my eyes from hers.

"Why did you do that?" she whispered, our gazes still locked.

I shrugged, telling her the truth. "I didn't want you to yell at me anymore."

"Oh." She lowered her eyes for a second.

"Livvy."

As soon as she heard her name, she raised her stare to me. With our gazes once again connected, I tucked a piece of her hair behind her ear.

"Are you still mad at me?"

"I don't think so."

"Good," was all I could reply.

I couldn't help myself and licked my lips, tasting what was left of her. Even though what I felt for her, what we felt for each other, wouldn't be understood until years later.

This was where it all began.

I didn't know it then, but that was when we started giving in to our love for one another.

This was only the beginning of our…

Friends-to-lovers relationship.

Chapter Three

LIVVY

SIXTEEN YEARS OLD

I'd ride my bike to our river in the woods often, just to have some peace and quiet. A secluded place where I could be alone with my thoughts and feelings. Away from my dad, who was suddenly riding my ass about college and what my SATs needed to be to gain admission into the universities he demanded I apply to.

I rode the dirt road to our special spot, wanting to clear my head with some exercise. Parking my bike near the willow tree, I grabbed my sunglasses, radio, and headphones from my backpack and headed to the water's edge. Slipping off my sandals near the shoreline, I walked through the tall grass into the murky, warm water. Letting the hot sun beam on me as I listened to the cricket's chirp.

I climbed onto the rope swing that hung just above the water off a willow branch. Ethan surprised me with it on my fifteenth birthday. Putting on my headphones next, I scrolled through my songs on my Spotify and found the tunes I was looking for. I started to swing to the soft melody of "Loving You" by The Canons while softly singing the lyrics to myself.

All of a sudden, the swing jerked back, almost sending me into the water. I let out a scream, turning to see who was behind me.

Ethan chuckled. "I like having you at my mercy."

"Don't you dare," I warned, instantly hopping off the swing. Kicking up water, I splashed him behind me.

He grinned in that Ethan, smart-ass sort of way. Cocking his head to the side, he challenged, "Don't start a war you can't win, Livvy."

"Oh yeah?" I never took my eyes off his as I tossed all my stuff beside my sandals on the shoreline so none of it would get wet.

With a shit-eating grin on my face, I leaned forward, building up the anticipation of what I was about to do. Pushing my hands through the water, I shoved a huge wave in his face.

He stepped back, his eyes widening in shock of what I'd just done. "Don't fuck with me," he goaded, hiding back a smile.

"I thought I already did." I splashed him again, this time with much more water in my hands. Not caring he was wearing all his clothes.

In a challenging expression, he bit, "Do that one more time and watch what happens, Livvy."

"Hmm..." I baited, placing my finger on the corner of my lips. "Watch me!"

I didn't give him a chance to reply before I went full force, splashing him as much as I could. Laughing my ass off the entire time, I never let up, throwing heaps of water at him. Each one worse than the last.

I vaguely heard him snap, "Don't say I didn't warn you."

"Wha—"

He threw me over his shoulder as if I weighed nothing, completely catching me by surprise. Holding the back of my knees, he kept me locked in place.

"Wait! What are you doing? This isn't fair! You're bigger than me!" I pressed my hands on his back to look up and see where he was carrying me.

He treaded deeper into the river, not caring he was getting his jeans soaked.

"No!" I screamed, fully aware of what he was going to do. "I don't want to go in there, Ethan! I'm wearing a nice dress! Please!" I pleaded, kicking and screaming.

His hands shifted to grip onto my waist, getting ready to do the unthinkable. I held him tighter, even though I knew it didn't matter, he was stronger than me.

"Begging won't help you in this situation. You should've thought of that before you decided you wanted to start a war with a guy who never loses."

"I'm sorry!" I apologized. "I was just playing! Put me down! Please!"

"Alright, but only because you asked so nicely."

I smiled, thinking I'd won. I couldn't have been more wrong. All of a sudden, he lifted me up by my waist, tearing my arms off him, and hurled me into the air like I was just a rag doll. I landed in the water, submerged under.

Coming up for air, I hollered, "You asshole!" I swam back toward him, stumbling to my feet once I could stand in knee-deep water. I looked down with my hands out at my sides. "Look!" I demanded. "Look what you did to my pretty white dress! I'm drenched because of you!"

I glared up at him, ready to give him hell as he stood in front of me, but the expression on his face rendered me speechless. His eyes roamed my soaking wet body. Beginning from my hips to my chest and up to my face with a predatory regard.

Our eyes locked, and he reached up, wiping a droplet of water off my cheek. His warm thumb stirred emotions deep inside me, causing my lips to part and my body to shudder.

I remembered the gleam in his eyes from when he kissed me, but as fast as it happened, it was gone. He shook it off, cleared his throat, and looked away from me. He rubbed the back of his neck, and an abrupt uncomfortable silence filled the air between us.

I followed the wake of his stare, peering down at my dress again. Finally realizing why he was taking me in so heatedly. The white flowy cotton clung to my body like a second skin, accentuating my curves and breasts. I wasn't wearing a bra and you could see-through the fabric, including the outline of my panties.

My nipples were hard with my legs slightly shaking. I swallowed hard, suddenly feeling exposed and vulnerable, but I didn't move to cover myself up. Reaching for the hem of his black shirt, he pulled it over his head and slid it off.

"Here," he stated, throwing it at me while still looking away.

I nodded even though he couldn't see me. After I was done putting it on, I giggled taking in my appearance. He faced me again, smiling at me. Just when I thought it couldn't get any more uncomfortable, I openly gawked at my best friend the same way he just did with me. His body was so tense from what just happened between us, showing off every sleek, toned muscle of his arms, sculpted chest, and carved abs, emphasizing his eight-pack.

His shoes were in the water, soaking the bottom of his jeans. The heaviness of the water dragged them down his slender waist, showing off his V right above his happy trail. Which, that in itself, was doing all sorts of things to me. He followed my open stare down to his exposed body, exactly the way I just did when he was ogling me.

Looking back up to my face, he pursed his lips, trying not to grin. It was my turn to look away from him although I didn't want to. My cheeks were flushed and my heart raced, rapidly beating hard against my chest and making me feel weak in the knees. His silence only made things more awkward between us.

"It's not the first time you're wearing my clothes," he reminded. "Half your closet is filled with my stolen hoodies."

I smirked. "You gave those to me."

He half smiled. "Expecting I'd get them back."

"You should have made that clear before you let me take them. Your clothes are always comfier than mine. Why do they always make guys clothes so much better than girls? You'd think it'd be the opposite."

"How many men's clothes are you wearing, Livvy?"

"Oh, you know... I don't kiss and tell."

He arched an eyebrow. "Yeah, well, you don't look bad wearing my clothes."

I blushed, not meeting his eyes as he placed his hands in the pockets of his jeans, simply accentuating his strong build.

"How did you know I was down here?" I asked, changing the subject.

He cleared his throat again, rasping in a hoarse tone, "Because I know my girl."

If he meant that in a possessive way, I didn't catch on. I was his girl. Always had been, always would be.

"Does that mean you followed me?"

He ignored my question. "Why the sad song, Livvy? Did one of your many guys break your heart today? Because I'll break their fucking legs."

I chuckled.

Over the past two years, the attention I received from boys probably changed the most about becoming a woman. I got asked out on a daily basis, but my dad's rule was that I wasn't allowed to date until I was seventeen. However, it didn't matter. I had no interest in any of them or anyone. It was always just Ethan and me, and I loved it that way. I didn't need the attention of other guys when I had him for that.

Ethan was also not interested in other girls. He never dated anyone or had a girlfriend. Not with us spending most of our time together. It didn't bother him. Girls were always trying to get him to notice them, but he wasn't ever affected by it. I think he was used to it at that point. If Ethan wasn't with me, then he kept his head in the books. You'd think studying was his job with the way he was constantly learning one thing or another.

It was almost like he had something to prove to himself, or maybe it was other people. My father still wasn't fond of him, and for some reason, it felt as if his disdain got worse as time passed. My mom and Ethan's uncle implemented a new rule: we weren't allowed in each other's rooms overnight. Now, we snuck in through our windows and locked our doors so we didn't get caught. It had yet to happen because we were very careful. We had too much to lose if we did.

I made my way over to my things by the shoreline and sat down, leaning back on my hands to leave my feet dangling in the water. Ethan followed, sitting beside me.

He nodded to his jeans and sneakers. "Look what you did."

"Serves you right."

With a grin, he nudged my shoulder with his. "You alright over there?"

I shrugged. "Why wouldn't I be?"

"Livvy, don't try me."

I smiled, peering up at him through my long, dark lashes. "It doesn't matter."

He spoke his truth...

"It does to me."

Chapter Four

LIVVY

Staring at the side of his face, I shrugged again, not knowing what to say until finally, I admitted, "Do you know what it's like to feel like your whole life is already planned out for you?"

"Your dad still giving you a hard time?"

"He's worse than ever." Sighing, I inhaled a deep breath.

"He just wants what's best for you."

"You always take his side."

"I'm always on your side."

"Except when it comes to him."

"It's not about sides when it comes to your old man, Livvy."

"Ethan," I adamantly stated, "he still doesn't like you. After ten years of our friendship, he still has something snarky to say when your name is mentioned. It's not fair. You can't be held responsible for the fact that your uncle isn't in his elite society, and I don't blame him for one second. They're all snobs, including my father."

"What your old man thinks of me has never bothered me. It is what it is."

"You're always so nonchalant about it."

"You're my best friend, and your dad isn't going to change that. Regardless of how much he thinks he will."

"So if your uncle was constantly bad-mouthing me, that wouldn't bother you?"

"That's different."

"How?"

"He's not my father," he simply stated, pausing for a second. "And I'm not going to come between the two of you."

I huffed another deep breath. "You're on the path of becoming the valedictorian of our graduating class, Ethan. Not to mention, you already have college credits, and we're only sophomores. What's it going to take for him to accept you as my best friend? You've more than proved your accomplishments to him, and it's still not good enough. All because your uncle doesn't wipe his ass with hundred-dollar bills."

His eyes sarcastically widened. "Now there's a visual I didn't want to see."

I chuckled. "You know what I mean."

He grinned. "I appreciate you wanting to stick up for me, but I don't need you to fight my battles."

"You're not fighting them, so somebody has to."

He shrugged it off. "Like I said, it is what it is."

"I hate it when you blow me off."

"I hate it that you still let this get to you when it shouldn't."

"So what, then? For the rest of my life, I'm just supposed to accept the fact that he thinks you're not good enough to be in mine?"

"It won't always be life this."

"How do you know?"

"I just do. You're just his baby girl, Livvy. He's simply doing his job like any good father would."

"Can you for once not be rational?" I sassed. "You're a great guy. He should be happy that my best friend is such an amazing person."

"Well, you remind him often enough."

"That's because I'm the only one who cares."

"I care about you, and that's all that matters to me."

"That's really sad." I disappointingly nodded. "You should be pissed."

"And what's that going to solve, huh?"

"I don't know, but it's better than not saying anything."

"What exactly am I supposed to say? He's your father. I'm not going to stir the pot when you do that enough for us both."

"Whatever." I rolled my eyes.

"He just wants what's best for you."

"Stop saying that! You're just making excuses for him."

"Livvy—"

Unable to bite my tongue, I confessed, "He wants me to go to Stanford University, Ethan. As in California. As in a five-hour plane ride. As in a forty-hour car ride from here. As in a whole-ass other coast away."

He jerked back. This was the first time I admitted this to him.

"Now that I got your attention," I mocked. "Why do you think that is?"

He was silent for a minute. It was obvious he was trying to gather his thoughts.

Shaking it off, he insisted, "It's a top school."

"Oh, come on!" I reprimanded. "You know it's because that college is the farthest away from you."

"Livvy, you don't know that."

"Trust me, I do. It doesn't matter how many scholarships you get. It won't matter. The tuition for that university is insane, and we both know you can't afford insane."

He didn't reply how I wanted him to. Instead, he asked, "What do you want me to say?"

Triggering me...

To snap.

ETHAN

"Why do you ask when you already know?"

"That's it." I gripped her thigh, tickling the shit out of her.

I was over her attitude. She instantly whipped around to no avail and finally gave up, laughing too hard to fight. I laughed too. Her laughter was always contagious. I fell over, onto her petite frame. It was only then I realized the compromising position we were suddenly in, and by the look in her eyes, she did too. I was now lying on top of her.

I smiled, looking down at her while she gazed up at me with an abrupt expression I couldn't quite read. There was so much emotion behind her eyes. I only ever saw it one other time, in this very same spot where we experienced our first kiss together. I pulled her hair away from her face, pinning it back behind her ears.

My hand caressed the side of her cheek, and I fucking knew I shouldn't be doing this, but I couldn't help myself. I grabbed the back of her neck, bringing her toward me and she came effortlessly. Her lips were just as I remembered, if not better. They tasted of honey-flavored lip gloss, and it stirred my dick in ways that now the mere smell of it would get me hard.

This was crazy.

This was my best friend.

This was Livvy.

What the hell is happening?

I sought out her tongue before she had the chance to find mine, needing to taste her, making her moan in my mouth. Both my hands found the sides of her face, and her hands found my hair, pulling at it. I took in the feel of her pouty lips while framing her face that I adored so fucking much before my hands began sliding down her body.

Fuck, she feels good.

Her wet dress had hiked up, exposing her thighs and silky smooth skin.

I needed to stop.

We needed to stop...

But I wanted nothing more than to keep going. Livvy had been the only girl I'd ever kissed, and I knew it was the same for her when it came to me. Our lips devoured each other as if we were both making a memory. I wish I could describe the intensity I felt with her in my arms. Only I couldn't even do it justice. I couldn't put into words what I felt in my heart.

What had always been there, to begin with.

It overpowered me. This was the second time I let it take control, and a huge part of me wanted to throw caution to the wind and just go with it.

I didn't.

I couldn't.

I enjoyed the sensation of her lips against mine one last time before I pulled away, causing her to whimper at the loss.

"Elizabeth," I breathed out, inches away from her mouth. My forehead set on hers, my hands holding the sides of her face.

She immediately opened her eyes. They appeared dark and dilated. I couldn't remember the last time I called her by her full name.

"Ethan," she panted back, luring me in again.

I softly pecked her lips, rubbing mine back and forth on hers.

"Please," she huskily pleaded, her tone soft and torn.

What is she asking for?

Does she even know?

"What do you—"

Her cell phone rang, cutting me off. We jumped at the sound, and I flew off her as she reached for her backpack to grab it.

"Dad," she answered. "Yeah, no, I know. I know, Dad. I'll be home soon. Okay, love you too." She hit end and sat up, and our eyes locked from the short distance between us.

Neither one of us said anything. Our intense gazes spoke for themselves.

"I have to go," she stated, breaking the silence.

I nodded.

"Okay." She got up first, and I quickly followed.

She walked her bike back to her house while I walked next to her. We were dead silent on the long hike to her home.

Once we were in front of her house, I announced, "I'll pick you up in the morning for school."

She nodded, not meeting my eyes.

I got my driver's license a few months ago, so I was basically her new chauffeur.

"You don't have to."

"I want to," I simply stated. "I'll see you in the morning." Stepping in, I kissed her cheek. "Sweet dreams, Livvy."

She half smiled. "Yeah, you too."

She made her way up the steps to the front door, and at the last second, before she opened it, she spun to look at me again. I nodded for her to go inside, and I didn't realize I still stood there when she looked out her bedroom window. I remained there with all the emotions and confusion wrapped around me like a vise.

Consuming me.

At that moment, I understood…

Livvy truly was my girl.

Chapter Five

LIVVY

EIGHTEEN YEARS OLD

Guys asked me to go to prom left and right, but I turned each one of them down. I decided I didn't want to go, so I didn't even bother buying a ticket. Something held me back from wanting to attend and enjoy the special night of my senior year. Something was missing, and I couldn't figure out what it was. The night every senior had been waiting for all our lives was finally here, and I'd be spending it on the couch, watching a horror movie.

Ethan just happened to be out of town, so I was alone for the evening. Our friendship was the same as always, nothing changed between us after we kissed. Throwing on one of his hoodies, I walked into the kitchen and ran into my dad. Not saying one word to him, I went to the fridge instead.

"How long are you going to continue the silent treatment toward me, Elizabeth?"

"Why does it matter?" I turned to face him. "You got what you wanted."

"I didn't want the silent treatment from my only baby girl."

"I'm not a baby anymore. I'm an adult who you still want to control."

"Wanting you to have the best education is not control."

"I could have the best education at South Carolina University too."

He narrowed his stare at me. "You really want to compare Stanford to SCU?"

"As a matter of fact, I do."

"You need to watch your tone, young lady."

I crossed my arms over my chest in defiance as he made his way over to me. When he stood in front of me, he rubbed the side of my head.

"I'm not going to apologize for wanting the best for you."

"And I'm not going to apologize for my attitude because of it."

He deeply sighed, cocking his head to the side. "One day, when you have your own kids, you'll understand where I'm coming from."

"I'd never force my child to go to a college they didn't want to attend."

"I guess time will tell, and we'll see about that."

I shook my head. "You don't understand me at all."

He stepped back, leaning against the kitchen island. "You think I don't understand you?"

"I know you don't."

"Alright…" He crossed his arms over his chest, mirroring my stance. "So if Ethan attended Stanford, you'd still have this objection of not wanting to go?"

I looked away. I had to.

"Yeah," he sternly replied, calling me out. "That's what I thought."

"You think I don't know he's the reason you want to send me away?"

"Send you away? Sweetheart, the last thing I'm doing is sending you away."

"Doesn't feel that way to me."

"Because you can't see further than the obsession you have with that boy."

"Let me remind you for the millionth time that boy is my best friend. Not an obsession."

"Elizabeth, you've never been on a date. Not. One. Single. Date. You've never had a boyfriend. I've never seen you around another guy who isn't Ethan Carter."

"You don't have to say his name with such disdain, you know?"

"I have no hate for a man I barely know."

"Exactly! You have never taken the time to get to know him, and last I remember, you didn't let me date until I was seventeen."

"That was over a year ago, and I have yet to see anyone show up to pick my daughter up for a date."

"You'd rather I date random guys than hang out with my best friend?"

"Don't twist my words, Elizabeth."

"You want to know about other guys, Dad? I'll tell you about all the other guys. All guys want is sex! That's all they think about. That's all they're into. Ethan is nothing like that. He's never been like that. You think just because he wasn't born with a silver spoon in his mouth that means he's not good enough to be in my life... News flash! All those country club boys who were born into pedigree families, they all suck even more!" I paused to catch my breath. "They don't think they're going to get laid, Dad. They expect it. All because of that damn silver spoon."

His arrogant expression faded as he quickly understood what I was sharing.

To add fuel to his already burning flame, I added, "But who knows, Daddy. Maybe I'll just make up for all the dates I'm not having in California. You know, make up for lost time."

He glared at me.

"What?" I played innocent. "I'm just doing what you want me to. Isn't that the point of all your parental demands?"

He snapped, "That's enough."

I reluctantly gave in, biting my tongue.

"Sweetheart, I love you very much."

Ugh! Great, now he's guilt-tripping me.

"All I want is what's best for you, and right now, attending one of the top schools in the world will set you up for life. Isn't that what you want? To have a nice life? Like the one I've given you."

"Being wealthy doesn't matter to me like it does to you."

"Oh, I see. You think that's it? That I just want to be rich?"

I shrugged. "If the shoe fits."

"You couldn't be more wrong. Do you have any idea how hard I work to give you and your mother the lives you deserve?"

"I never asked for this life. I'd be happy to have you around more than to have you be a slave to your career."

He jerked back.

"I'm not trying to hurt your feelings, Daddy. I'm just…" I lingered, trying to gather my words so that he could try to understand where I was coming from. "I don't want to pick up my entire life and start in a brand-new state and town where I don't know anybody. I'll be completely alone, and I can't believe you'd prefer that for me, just to keep me away from Ethan."

"Elizabeth—"

"You know it's true. Why can't you just admit that to yourself?"

With a stern voice, he bit, "I don't have to explain myself to you. I know what's best, and that's for you to attend Stanford."

"Whatever."

"We'll just have to agree to disagree, understood?"

"I guess."

He opened his mouth to respond, but the doorbell rang, cutting him off.

"Saved by the bell," I muttered under my breath on my way to answer it.

When I did, I never expected who'd be standing there wearing a black tuxedo with a corsage in his hand.

ETHAN

Livvy was oblivious to any attention thrown her way. The magnetic pull she had toward guys was unbelievable, and I spent most of her eighteenth birthday fighting them off at the club. Her natural beauty was a lure. They could smell that shit from a mile away.

Livvy knew I'd be out of town, and when she told me she wasn't going to prom because she wasn't feeling it, I knew it was a bunch of bullshit. Since we were kids, she talked about stupid high school stuff like the prom. She called them milestones and memories to last a lifetime.

I called her mom and asked her to buy her the gown I'd seen her save on her cell phone one night, and I took care of the rest. This year had been hard on her. She'd be moving to California at the end of the summer, and we'd start two completely different lives from one another for the first time since we met on the school bus all those years ago.

It was hard for me too.

I hated that she would be alone.

I hated that she would be so far away.

I hated that I wouldn't see her every day.

The list of all the things I hated about her attending Stanford was endless.

Her mom, however, was more than willing to help in any way she could. Ecstatic that Livvy would have a beautiful memory from her last year of high school. I rented a tuxedo that matched her white lace gown.

The look on her face was priceless as soon as she opened the door.

That was all the reassurance I needed.

"Ethan," she greeted, surprised I stood there before her. "You look, oh my God, you look amazing. What are you doing here?"

I smiled. "I'm here for you."

"I thought you had to go to Kansas with your uncle for the weekend."

"You're more important to me, Livvy. So I'm here to be your knight in shining armor. Allow me the honor of taking you to the prom."

With wide, teary eyes, she conveyed, "What?"

"You heard me."

"But... I don't have anything to wear. I don't even have tickets." She looked down at herself. "I mean, look at me. I'm a mess."

"I am looking." I loved seeing her in my clothes. "You're always perfect, but your mom—"

Right on cue, her mother opened the door a little farther. "Ethan, you look amazing. So handsome."

"Thank you, Mrs. Collins."

Livvy peered back and forth between us, catching on without us having to say anything.

"Honey, your dress is on your bed," Mrs. Collins shared. "I laid it out for you, along with the heels I bought for it."

"You two were in cahoots?"

I winked at her. "I took care of the rest."

"What about Dad?"

Her mom smiled. "Don't worry about your father. I already warned him not to ruin this for you."

Livvy instantly threw her arms around her. "Thank you, Mom. I'm so lucky to have you."

"And don't you ever forget that."

Livvy beamed, letting out a loud shriek before she ran up the stairs. I waited in the living room for her, but it didn't take long for her old man to show up. The sound of him clearing his throat made me turn around. He stood under the archway, all tall and intimidating. I figured he was about to start the "prom conversation."

Don't touch my daughter.

Have her home by a certain time.

No drinking.

Be responsible, and so on.

"Hello, Mr. Collins."

He nodded to the couch. "Have a seat, Ethan. I'd like to talk to you for a minute."

"Sure," I breathed out, sitting beside him, turning to give him my full attention.

This was the most he'd ever said to me, and I couldn't help but feel anxious.

"I can't believe how fast time has gone by."

I nodded, taking in his words and mentally gearing myself up. I braced myself for what was to come. It wouldn't be what I expected. It'd be much worse. They say everything happens for a reason, that we're destined to meet certain expectations throughout the timeline of our lives. They're inevitable. It's already planned out.

If that were true, then this would be the beginning of the end for us. It always started and ended with her old man.

"I don't think I need to tell you how I feel about your friendship with my daughter?"

I shook my head. "No, sir."

He eyed me up and down, trying to read me and my reaction to him. I held my ground. I'd never disrespect him, and it was obvious he was trying to have a man-to-man conversation with me. I owed him enough to listen.

"Elizabeth needs to experience new things and grow up, Ethan. All she knows is you. I don't have to tell you that, do I?"

"All I have is her too."

He tapered his stare at me. "You both need to experience new things without each other. It's not healthy to only have one another."

I didn't know what to say, so I kept my mouth shut. Instead, I set my elbows on my knees and bowed my head.

I know.

I knew it all.

I knew everything and where this was going…

Chapter Six
ETHAN

"You know Livvy as well as we do. She's stubborn and hardheaded. It doesn't matter how many times we've tried to talk to her. She won't listen to us. We've spent the entire school year trying to get through to her, but nothing. It doesn't matter what we say, she's going to feel the way she wants."

"I understand, sir."

"Do you? Because I don't think you do."

"Sir, I—"

"Do you know she applied to SCU?"

I jerked back. I didn't know that. "Now why do you think that is?"

I didn't have to answer him. He knew I was aware of why she'd apply there. I had a free ride to South Carolina University. I'd be a fool not to go there. As much as I wanted to be with her and despite getting accepted to Stanford, I couldn't afford it.

He read my mind. "I didn't think so. It's been hard for her mother and me to watch her this year. It would hurt any parent to watch their child suffer from something they can't understand is in their best interest, which is why I'm hoping that you can help us."

I angrily shut my eyes, bile rising up in my throat, but I swallowed it back down. I wasn't mad at him. I wasn't mad at Livvy. I was mad at myself. Nothing would change what he expected me to do. It didn't matter. I knew what I needed to do even though it was the furthest thing from what I wanted. He was right, though. I couldn't ignore that fact.

He's right.

His words made a mockery of me, and I knew that too.

"I know you care for Livvy. You wouldn't be sitting here if you didn't. That's why, I know you'll do the right thing and let her find her own way. Not follow yours. Do you understand me, Ethan?"

I slightly nodded, keeping my emotions in check.

"I want my daughter to be independent and make her own choices, decide what's right for her, and she can't do that with you around. You know that as well, right?"

I vaguely nodded again, not being able to form words or even coherent thoughts for that matter.

"I hope you understand where I'm coming from." His hand burned when he placed it on my shoulder, leaving a scar for the future that didn't include her.

"Maybe tonight can be the closing of one door, but the opening of another. For both of you."

I heard the clicking of heels on the hardwood floor and immediately stood, turning to see her. I'd never seen Livvy look more gorgeous than she did in that second. The dress fit her exactly how I imagined. Her hair flowed loosely down her face and back. Her makeup was subtle, accenting her perfect, precise features, and I could smell her honey lip gloss from across the room.

She's breathtaking.

"Livvy," I stammered as she shyly smiled.

Her mom snapped picture after picture, and then we left.

"Come on." I placed my hand on the hollow of her back, spreading a warm heat throughout my entire body as I guided her toward the door of my truck.

She tried to step up on the ladder, but her heels wouldn't allow it. I grabbed her waist from behind and lifted her instead. Shutting the door behind her, I rounded the hood and jumped in next. We drove in silence to the dance. Before I knew it, we walked through the doors of the banquet hall that hosted our prom.

Decorations seemed to go on for miles, as did the crowd. Every inch of the room was covered in some sort of streamer, confetti, or balloon. We took our traditional prom picture with the photographer, but she didn't get a chance to look at it since I immediately placed it inside my tuxedo jacket.

I grabbed her hand, and I didn't give it any more thought as she followed me into the ballroom. We hung out like we always did, laughing and loving each other's company. We always had our own dynamic, living in our own little world where nothing or nobody mattered but us.

When Livvy excused herself to use the restroom, I leaned against the wall to look at how everyone appeared to be happy and in love. I wondered if we looked like that from an outside perspective. My question was answered when I heard one of her favorite songs play through the speakers, "Simple Man" by Lynyrd Skynyrd.

I glanced around until I found Livvy with a smug grin on my face, waiting for her to meet me on the dance floor. I softly sang it to her as I held her in my arms, spinning her in circles and bringing her close to my chest to the rhythm of the music. I wanted no space between us. She laid her head on my chest, and I placed my chin on top of her head, softly singing the lyrics to her again. It was around the chorus of the song when something felt different.

She felt different.

She stared deep into my eyes and said, "Let's get out of here."

And I didn't have to wonder where we'd go.

LIVVY

Thirty minutes later, he parked his truck at our river. The rumbling of the diesel engine hummed beneath our bodies for a moment before he grabbed the blanket he kept in the back seat, and we moved to sit on the bed of his truck. I stared at the water that stored so many memories and firsts for us. Except we weren't kids anymore.

We were adults.

Man and woman.

About to embark on a journey without each other.

The truth was, I was terrified to lose him. I couldn't imagine my life without him, and I didn't want to pretend this wasn't absolutely killing me inside. I felt as if my father was tearing out my insides, stealing my breath a little more with every passing second. I wish I could make him understand or at least be sympathetic. It was no use. It was a war I never had a chance of winning.

Neither one of us said anything for what felt like an eternity until finally, he broke the silence, asking, "Why didn't you tell me you applied to SCU?"

"I don't know."

"Bullshit."

I leaned my head against the headrest. "I thought I'd attend without his blessing."

He turned to face me. "Livvy, why?"

"What do you mean why? You know I want to be with you. I thought we could—"

"No," he firmly stated, immediately making me turn to look at him.

"No?" I repeated, confused.

"You're not going there because of me. You're not giving up Stanford because of me."

"Why not?"

"Because you're just following me."

"So what if I am?"

He bowed his head in defeat, and I wanted to crawl into his lap and make it all go away. Exactly how I always did when he was sad.

"You can't follow me," he let out. I didn't want to hug him anymore; now I just wanted to scream at him.

"You can't tell me what to do!"

He scoffed, "The fuck I can't."

I fervently shook my head. "You don't mean that. I want to be with you, and I know you want me to be there too."

He shut his eyes like he was trying to make me disappear. I wouldn't grant him that leniency.

"At least look at me if you're going to break my heart, Ethan. I deserve at least that, don't I?"

He shut his eyes tighter, and I didn't back down.

"I love you, Ethan."

I didn't recognize the guy sitting next to me with a bowed head and distant demeanor.

He wasn't my Ethan.

My boy.

My best friend.

Ethan wouldn't hurt me. He wouldn't break my heart and not have the decency to look me in the eyes as he did it. Making me bleed out for him.

"I thought you loved me too."

"I do."

"Then what's the problem? I don't need my father's approval on where I go to college and what I do with my future."

"It isn't your future, Livvy. It's mine."

"Then why did you apply to Stanford, huh? I know it wasn't because you liked the campus. You did it because you want to be with me too. Just admit it. What did my father say to you that's making you pull away from me now?"

The hollow feeling built inside me. The emptiness surged from my heart throughout my entire body, causing me to feel like I was broken and truly alone.

Like something was wrong with me.

I had nothing left to say, nothing left for me to do. I don't know how long we sat there, both of us lost in our thoughts and disillusions when I did the only thing left for me to save the future of our friendship.

I climbed in his lap, straddling his waist...

And kissed him.

Chapter Seven

ETHAN

Ever so lightly, she pecked my lips, and as much as I wanted to resist her, I couldn't.
I won't.
Instead, I willingly gave in and followed her lead. This was the first time Livvy initiated a kiss between us. After all this time, she was still the only girl I'd ever done this with, and it hadn't changed for her either. I was the only man to ever touch her lips. Never had I thought we'd kiss like this. Our tongues weren't touching, but it still felt like the most intimate kiss of my entire life.

The second her tongue touched mine, I felt my cock stir. Once again, driven by a pure impulse like the last two times, I gripped the back of her neck and dragged her toward me as if she wasn't already close enough. This was only our third kiss, but it didn't matter. It was enough. I pulled her closer to my mouth. Her eyes never left mine, and I took control the moment our lips touched again.

I teased her with the tip of my tongue, gliding it all along the outline of her pouty mouth. The feel of her silky tongue was like nothing I'd ever felt before. Our movements were in sync with one another.

It was easy.
Natural.
Home.

I pecked her one last time until I rested my forehead against hers as we breathed heavily.

I grinned. Her stare was dark and dilated, luring me in to want to kiss her again. Her long, messy hair draped all around her face cascaded all around us. Our gaze stayed connected as if we were trying to burn this moment into our memories. Sweeping her hair away from her face, I brushed my lips against hers, side to side.

"What are we doing, Livvy?"

"I don't know, what we've been doing for the last four years."

"Do you want me to stop?"

"No."

"Do you want me to keep going?"

"Yes."

"How far do you want me to take this?" My pounding heart mirrored hers. I could feel it rapidly beating against my chest.

She answered my question with another long, passionate kiss before I could assure her how much she meant to me, how much she always meant to me. To tell her what I felt so deeply in my heart...

My best friend.

My family.

My girl.

I replied the only way I knew how—I kissed her back, letting myself get lost with her.

Panting against my mouth, she coaxed, "Just keep going, and we'll find out together."

I slowly moved my hands up her body, feeling the softness of her skin through her dress. Her breath hitched when my body fell forward, pushing her back onto the bed of my truck to lay between her thighs. Placing all my weight on my arms, I cradled her face, and we made out like two crazy teenagers who couldn't get enough of each other. I never wanted to stop kissing her.

Holding her.

Being on top of her.

My eyes followed the movement of her hands when she reached for my tuxedo jacket, pulling it off and discarding it next to us. She beckoned me to continue down this uncharted territory between us. I groaned in satisfaction. Second by second, I deliberately took it slow. Confidently crawling my way down her body, I lightly skimmed my lips across the top of her breasts, igniting tingles all over her skin against my lips.

She then reached for the bottom of her dress, locking heady stares with me. I didn't stop her when she lifted it off her body, leaving her only in her panties. This was the first time I saw her topless; this was the first time I saw any girl topless who wasn't in a movie or magazine.

I swallowed hard, never expecting this drastic turn in our friendship, but appreciating it nonetheless.

"Jesus, you're fucking gorgeous, Livvy."

All she begged was, "Don't stop."

And I didn't have to be told twice. Sucking her nipple into my mouth, I watched as her back arched off the bed, and she fisted the blanket. Her body pleaded with me to keep going, and I happily obliged.

I gave her what she wanted.

What we both desperately wanted.

Kissing my way down her stomach, my predatory glare never left her eyes as I continued my tour of her petite frame.

"Should I keep going?"

Through the slits of her heated gaze, she nodded.

"Just so we're clear... you want me to kiss you"—I grinned—"down there?"

She blushed.

"You're going to get all shy on me now? I'm barely hanging on by a thread here."

"My shyness is turning you on?"

"Among other things."

"Take my panties off, Ethan."

"Oh, so now you're giving me orders?"

She giggled, and again, I didn't have to be told twice. I tugged her panties down her long, luscious legs, making a mental note of how delicious she fucking looked. My eyes scanned her sexy body, greedily devouring every last inch of her soft skin. I started from her rosy cheeks down to her perfectly flushed, perky tits to her round hips and slender thighs. Right down to where my eyes wanted to see the most.

Her pussy.

"Will you spread your legs for me, Livvy?"

Almost like she was opening a gift for me, she slowly did as she was told, and through hooded eyes, I watched her every move. There was no hesitation whatsoever when I took her in.

She was pink.

Wet.

Perfect.

Before I could contemplate what we were doing, I licked from her opening to her clit.

"Oh God." Her eyes rolled to the back of her head.

I watched enough porn to know what to do. If there was one thing about me, I loved to learn new things and be prepared for everything. She moaned, fluttering her heated gaze on me. Our stares locked, and she watched as I licked from the bottom to the top of her slit. She just about came undone when my tongue flicked her clit.

"Tell me what you like," I ordered, sucking her clit into my mouth. "Do you like that?"

She didn't say a word. I could barely hear her breathing.

"Or..." I sucked it again, moving my head side to side. "Like that."

She loudly moaned that time, which earned her a smile. I didn't even try to hide it.

"You like that?"

"Yeah..."

I continued my sweet torture with my tongue on her clit, and she rocked her hips against what I was doing. A whimper escaped her lips as I dove my tongue as far as it would go into her core, loving the taste of her. She melted against my tongue, into my touch, coming apart from everything I was doing. Sucking her clit harder and faster, I was relentless in my pursuit to have her come for me.

"Oh God... right there. Please... right there..."

"Right there?" I mocked, pushing her over the edge.

Her back arched off the bed again, fisting the sheet so hard that her knuckles started turning white. Her impending orgasm completely consumed her.

"Stop talking and... right there..."

"Here?"

"Oh God, yes—there..."

"You feel that?" I huskily groaned, appreciating the sight and feel of her getting off.

She was close, almost there. I could tell by her frenzied movements and erratic breathing. She couldn't wait any longer. Within seconds, her legs started to shake, and she couldn't keep her eyes open. Her hands immediately gripped my hair, and I grunted in pleasure.

"Hmm ... ah ... mmm..." she exhaled, coming...

Long.

Hard.

Fast.

All the way down my chin.

I smiled, feeling damn proud of myself. Licking my lips, I wiped my chin with the back of my hand before inching my way up her body. I stopped when I was at her face.

"How was that?"

She smiled wide with her eyes still shut. "That was amazing."

"Yeah, it was."

She opened her gaze, and all I could see were dark pools of ecstasy as she reached for my belt. My eyebrows pinched together, looking down at her hands.

"Livvy—"

"Just be with me, Ethan."

I'd be lying if I said I didn't expect her to add...

"It was always going to be you."

Chapter Eight

ETHAN

"Are you sure?"

"I've never been more sure of anything in all my life."

"I don't think—"

"Please... Just be with me."

"I don't have a condom."

"It's fine. I'm on the pill."

My eyes widened. "Are we really going to do this?"

"You don't want to?"

"Of course I want to."

"Then what's stopping you?"

"You have to have sex for the first time like this? Here?"

"I can't think of a better spot. This is our place, Ethan. It's always been ours."

She was right. It was.

Not considering the consequences, I gave in to her immediately. Unbuttoning my collared shirt, I slid it off with my belt, pants, and boxer briefs next.

She glanced down my body, her stare falling right on my hard cock. "Shit."

"What?"

"Your dick is huge. Why didn't you ever tell me that?"

I arched an eyebrow. "You really want to have this conversation right now?"

"Yeah." She hesitantly smiled. "That thing is going to break me."

I laughed. I couldn't help it. She was fucking adorable. Not wanting to discuss my cock anymore, I claimed her mouth again, aggressively kissing her. Positioning my cock at her entrance, I held it there.

Between kissing her, I muttered, "If we do this, it's going to change everything between us."

"Promise?"

"Livvy, I don't want to fuck up our friendship. It's too important to me."

"We won't. Our friendship will always come first, Ethan. No matter what."

Her reassurance was what I needed to hear to keep going.

"Maybe we're best friends that have sex with each other this summer?"

I chuckled, pecking her lips. "Like friends with benefits?"

"Yeah," she panted, sliding her tongue in my mouth.

"I don't think that's going to work."

"Why?"

I slid my tongue past her lips. "Because it's you."

She giggled, and my cock twitched.

"Let's stop talking now and just be with me, Ethan."

Nothing compared or even came close to the feeling of my girl, to the sensations she stirred inside me. This was more than just sex, more than just two bodies coming together, more than anything I ever thought I'd experienced before.

This was her.

My best friend.

"There's no coming back from this."

She agreed, "I know."

"I don't want to hurt you, so tell me if I am, okay?"

She nodded.

"You're so fucking beautiful," I groaned, wanting to claim every inch of her body.

She bit her bottom lip as I gently pushed in, the feel of her wrapped around me, inch by inch, was immediate and almost too much to bear. I could tell I was hurting her by the expression on her face and I reached down to rub her already sensitive clit, trying to make it better for her. Her breathing hitched and her lips parted, making her pussy that much tighter.

"Are you okay?" I thrust in a little more.

"Mmm..." That was all she could reply.

"I'm almost there. Fuck, Livvy, you're so fucking tight."

I took a moment when I was fully inside her, leaning back to look at her, wanting to remember her just this way, always.

Her long, silky brown hair spread all over.

The way her cheeks were slightly flushed and how the blush crept down to her neck.

How her lips were swollen from my assault and her serene eyes glazed over.

So beautiful.

So fucking beautiful.

I placed a soft kiss on the pulse on her neck, loving the feel of it beating against my lips. I positioned my knee a little higher, causing her leg to incline with mine. Her breathing spiked, and I knew I would hit her G-spot better from that angle.

My face hovered above hers as we caught our breath, trying to find a rhythm. It was effortless, the two of us coming together. My thrusts began, gentle at first.

"Are you okay?"

"Yes... Stop worrying about me."

Easier said than done.

Her body responded perfectly with mine. I lapped at her breasts, unable to get enough of her.

"Ethan," she breathed out, and I swear my cock got harder.

I moved back up to her face, and our mouths parted, we both panted profusely. We stayed like that for I don't know how long, completely consumed with one another until I began to feel myself starting to come apart.

"Fuck, you feel good. How do you feel this good?"

"Mmm..." I moaned, her pussy gripping my dick.

I played with her clit faster, harder. Trying to get her to come again with me inside her. Once I felt her climax and heard her scream my name, she took me along. I shook with my release and passionately kissed her.

From her neck.

To her breasts.

Back up to her lips.

I didn't know where we went from here. There was no going back after this. We crossed the line. I didn't have the answers because I barely knew the questions.

She was my best friend, and I loved her. I'd always loved her.

I watched my life flash before my eyes.

Our memories.

Our childhood.

Our firsts.

Was this our last?

The past.

The present.

The future…

Livvy needed to experience new things. I couldn't stand in her way. It wouldn't be fair. Her father was right. I was so fucking confused.

Suddenly, she professed, "All we have is this summer, Ethan. Can we make it worthwhile?"

She didn't have to elaborate. I had no choice in the matter, so my heart spoke for me…

"I can't think of one fucking reason to say no."

"Ah…" she stirred awake, arching her back off the bed as my thumb pulled her hood, exposing her bright red clit.

My mouth immediately assaulted it with a forceful sucking motion as I started eating her pussy for breakfast.

"Holy shit…" she panted in a sleepy but sexy voice, gripping the sheets above her head.

I woke up hard and hungry for her. Not thinking twice about sliding underneath the blankets in a slow, steady pace, I crawled my way toward her core like a starved man. Before she knew what I was doing, my face was buried between her legs, savoring what was officially mine for the taking.

Time sped by, and it was already almost two months into the summer. This was how we spent most of our time. There weren't many places or positions we hadn't tried at that point. I guess you could say we were making up for lost time.

"Ethan, we can't..."

I sucked her clit harder, moving my head faster.

"Keep doing this... oh, God..."

Side to side, up and down, I was relentless in my pursuit of her come. Seeing how fast I could get her to drip down my face became a challenge.

"How are you so good at that?"

I hummed, releasing her nub with a loud pop. If I was good at one thing, it was paying attention to what she loved. Her body was so unbelievably responsive to my touch. There wasn't an inch of her skin I hadn't kissed or memorized. Down to every last freckle on her face, neck, breasts, and she even had some near and on her pussy.

I softly blew on her clit. "I know my girl."

Our stares locked when I slid two fingers inside her warm, welcoming heat, aiming them right toward her G-spot.

"You want me to stop?" I teased.

"Ah... I'm just saying..."

I moved my fingers back and forth, slow at first, before building up her wetness of coming apart. I could read Livvy like a fucking book, and sex with her was no different. If anything, I think this was where I excelled the most.

"We've... been having sex nonstop... I mean... I'm not complain...ing or anything, but... oh, God... two, three times a day... might be... a little... much..."

"Are you going to come for me?" I rasped with a grin, sucking her clit back between my lips while ignoring everything she tried to say.

"Okay..." she replied, grinding her pussy against my mouth and swaying her hips in the opposite direction of the up-and-down movement of my head.

My mouth sent her into a frenzy as I took my time devouring her sweet pussy.

Forcefully.

Urgent.

All consuming.

Chapter Nine

ETHAN

Her legs started to shake from the mere graze of my tongue, making her nice and drenched for me. She was almost there. "I'm... going to... come..." she whimpered in uncontrollable pleasure.

My hands moved to her breasts, kneading her hard nipples while lapping at her pussy. It didn't take long for the tingling sensation to develop all over her body. I could feel it through the goose bumps of her silky skin. She placed her foot on my shoulder and started riding the fuck out of my face, and seconds later, she came in my mouth.

I growled, roughly holding her down.

"It's too much, Ethan... I can't..."

I didn't let up, wanting her to continue to lose her mind until finally, I granted her the mercy she sought. Kissing her clit one last time, she jolted from being overly stimulated.

"What did I do to deserve this kind of wake-up call?" she breathlessly panted as I climbed up her body. "I feel like I should say thank you or something?"

I grinned. "No need to thank me. I did that for me."

"Well then." She smiled. "At least let me return the favor."

She rolled us over, and now she was on top of me, sitting directly on my hard cock and making it twitch.

I licked my lips, still tasting her in my mouth. Placing my hands on her bare ass, I subtly rubbed my thumbs up and down. Having Livvy naked, all flush and warm, and ready with her tits in my face was a vision I'd never forget.

I couldn't keep clothes on her. She was either nude, in my shirts, or in tiny tank tops with panties that always showed the bottom of her ass cheeks. Not that I was complaining. I loved it when she wore my clothes instead of hers. Something about her wearing what belonged to me made my cock throb and my mind wander to the things I'd do to her once I got it off.

"As much as I'd love to see you on your knees with my cock in your mouth. We have other plans for today."

"Plans?" She cocked her head to the side. "Oh, I see what this was." She smirked, sassing, "You were trying to weasel your way out of forgetting to tell me we were going somewhere."

I laughed. "Didn't you just say that we couldn't keep doing this all day?"

"Hmm..." She thought about it for a moment. "Now what?"

LIVVY

"What sorts of fun stuff do you have planned for us?"

"First, I thought I'd feed you, and maybe if you're a really good girl, I'll even take you to a movie." He smirked.

"Like on a date?"

"Maybe."

"Have I told you how much I love that my parents and your uncle are out of town at the same time? I didn't have to sneak into your window last night, and I got to spend the night."

"I do love these sleepovers."

"Right? Just think about it." She wiggled her eyebrows. "Soon, we'll be living in our own places, and we can have sleepovers when we visit each other."

The airiness in the room instantly shifted into unanswered questions we'd yet to ask one another. Since prom, we were literally living our best lives together. For the first time, we kissed, held hands, and touched each other whenever we wanted. The list was endless of all the ways we explored this new world of sex between us.

Not only were we both virgins to begin with but it only added to the excitement of trying out all these new positions and places we could together. Granted, it was just two months since we started this new sexual dynamic, but that didn't matter. We'd probably had sex at least a hundred times. Ethan spent more time inside me than not.

I couldn't tell you how much fun it was. Being able to be free in this way was everything. We went from friends to lovers like it was the easiest thing in the entire world.

It felt natural.

Simple.

Except summer was almost over. Soon, we'd be heading in different directions. Miles and hours apart. A whole other life. I tried not to think about the looming end of us.

This has to end, right?

We hadn't spoken about the future or where we went from there. We would forever be best friends. That wasn't the issue. The main question was...

Can we be more?

Unable to hold it in any longer, I blurted, "Ethan, what are we doing?"

"Well, currently, you're naked on top of me."

I chuckled. "You know what I mean."

"Livvy, if you want to have a serious conversation, then I'm going to need you to put some clothes on because all I can focus on right now is how much I want to bend you over the bed and fuck you doggy style."

"They're just boobs. You're such a guy." I grabbed the sheet, covering myself. "Better?"

"Hardly. Your wet pussy is still on my hard cock."

I shook my head. "Can you please focus for five minutes?"

"As much as it pains me to say this, I'm going to need you to get off me. I can't think straight with you sitting on me naked. The white sheet only makes you sexier. You're like a present I want to unwrap."

"Oh my God!" I jumped off, but right before I could step off the bed. He grabbed the back of my neck and kissed me like we weren't about to have the inevitable discussion.

"You're so fucking gorgeous," he breathed out against my lips.

"You always know the right things to say."

"I only speak the truth." With that, he let me go.

I grabbed his hoodie from the floor, throwing it on with my panties next, and then turned around to look at him.

"Is this more of what you had in mind?"

"Not really, but it'll do."

After he slid his gym shorts on, he sat against the headboard while I sat on the edge of the bed.

"Why so far away?"

"If I go near you, then one thing leads to another, and you know… you're insatiable."

"Only when it comes to you."

With a smile, I repeated, "What are we doing?"

"In reference to what?"

I pointed back and forth between us. "To this."

"We're best friends."

"I know that, but then we're just what? Best friends with benefits?"

"Isn't that what you wanted?"

"Yeah…"

"Then what's the problem?"

"So then this is just a summer fling?"

"Livvy, you're far from a fling or even just a fuck. I love you."

"I love you too."

"I know. What happens after this summer?"

"You move to California."

"Right…" I bowed my head. "And when you visit or when I do, are we just going to pick up where we left off?"

He shrugged. "I don't know."

"Yeah," I agreed, nodding. "I don't know either."

"Is that what you want? To pick up where we left off?"

"Do you?"

"Livvy, I just want you in my life, and I'll take you in whatever way I can."

I nodded again. "Me too, but does that mean... we're just going to go back to being best friends, and this was just a phase in our friendship?"

"You'll never just be a phase for me. You'll always be my girl, regardless of where life takes us."

"As in girlfriend?"

His eyebrows tightly pinched together, and it was enough for me to completely retreat.

"Never mind." I abruptly stood. "Forget I said anything."

Before I could walk away, he grabbed my wrist and pulled me toward him. He peered deep into my eyes once he had my face between his hands.

"I can't just put a label on you, Livvy. Any more than I can just put a label on us. You're so much more than any word could ever explain what you mean to me. Girlfriend doesn't begin to describe who you are in my life. Do you understand what I'm saying?"

"I think I do."

"If you're asking me if I plan on being with anyone after you move, then the answer is no. Now if you're asking me if I plan on you being with anyone after you move, then the answer is I'll break his fucking legs if you do."

I giggled. I couldn't help it.

"Does that answer your questions?"

I beamed, feeling so much better. "Yes."

He didn't waver in replying...

"Good."

Chapter Ten
LIVVY

He drove to our first destination, which was the zoo and aquarium. Guiding me through the animals, he held my hand the entire time of our private behind-the-scenes tour that he surprised me with. Ethan knew how much I loved animals. It didn't matter what kind it was. If it was furry, I was obsessed with it.

"Aw! Look at the babies. I want to take one home," I expressed, looking inside the lion cub cages.

"Want to hold one?"

I immediately looked back at him with a confused expression on my face.

"I'll take that as a yes." He chuckled, nodding behind me.

Out of nowhere, a man appeared, opening the gates for us to follow. We had to stay in the corner until he brought one of the cubs over to us.

"This is Meiko. He's four months old," the trainer informed us, setting him down on the ground.

I crouched down to pet him, and he wouldn't stop licking my hand.

"Meiko loves the ladies," he added, making me laugh.

"Hey, Meiko," Ethan stated. "This one is mine."

I rolled my eyes, enjoying his possessiveness, even with a lion.

Ethan snapped pictures of us with his phone before we moved into the huge circular aquarium.

"Wow," I exclaimed, letting go of Ethan's hand. I walked around in utter amazement at all the colors of the fish and sea life. "They're so beautiful. Oh, I love this one!"

"That's a Clarion angelfish."

"I love this one, too!"

"That's a koi."

"What about that one?"

"A regal tang."

I pointed at hundreds, and he knew each one.

"How did you know that?"

"I learned it in a book."

"Is there anything you don't know?"

He laughed me off, but it was a genuine question. Ethan was a wealth of knowledge, and I couldn't believe how much it turned me on. After we finished our tour, he took me to get ice cream. I had such a sweet tooth. It was a running joke that I could probably live off sweets if needed.

That was one of the things I loved the most about Ethan. He always paid attention to all the little things. He could turn any situation into a loving one that usually left me in awe of him.

"Where are we going now?" I asked as he took the exit for the highway.

"Can't I surprise you?"

I raised my eyebrow and cocked my head to the side.

"Yeah... good point," he recognized.

I smiled.

"Your birthday is coming up."

"My birthday isn't for another few months."

"I'm aware of when your birthday is," he stated, reaching for my thigh, but I intercepted his hand at the last second.

"Ohhh! Did you see that, big man? Gotta be quicker than that. I have cat-like reflexes."

"What was that?" he mocked, quickly gripping my inner thigh. "I'm sorry, I didn't catch that? Cat-like what?"

I thrashed, squealing and laughing all at the same time until he finally let go.

Once I caught my breath, I questioned, "Now you were saying."

"You mean before I was rudely interrupted?"

"Yes, before that."

He looked at me, grinning.

"Look where you're driving before you crash."

He smiled, once again content. "Consider this a pre-celebration for your nineteenth birthday."

He grabbed my hand, holding it in his lap for the rest of the ride to wherever he was taking me.

ETHAN

Watching the way Livvy's eyes widened as she took in the beauty of this place was a sight I'd never forget. I was doing this for her, but I was also doing it for myself. The expression on her face was worth making her wait to know what I was surprising her with.

I watched as she walked over the wooden bridge in the center of the flower garden to get a better view of all the flowers and roses. Her enticing bright green eyes glanced back at me over her shoulder, and I couldn't gather a fucking thought. I'd never seen her look more beautiful than I did at that moment. The light of the shining sun heightened her features, emphasizing the freckles across her button nose and sculpted cheeks.

She's stunning.

All these emotions I wasn't expecting crept into the forefront of my mind, and I couldn't control any of them. After all these years, all this time, Livvy didn't look like my best friend, but like a woman I was seeing for the first time.

Right there.

In that second, I wanted more.

I wanted it all.

She was gorgeous, with her hair flowing loosely around her face. Although her beauty captured my attention, it was the expression on her face that consumed me the most. I'd seen Livvy in all forms.

Happy.

Sad.

Devastated.

Excited.

There wasn't an emotion, a time, a memory that didn't involve her in it in one way or another. However, I'd never seen her quite like this...

She stood against the railing with her lips slightly parted, and I wanted to know what she was thinking. What she was feeling.

"This is simply incredible, Ethan. How have we never been here before? I didn't even know this place existed."

My feet moved on their own accord until I suddenly stood behind her. Her breathing hitched as soon as she felt my chest against her back.

She didn't turn around.

She didn't move.

I wasn't sure she was even breathing.

For a minute, I breathed her in. I felt the heat of her body burning into me more and more with each second that passed between us. Leaning in, just inches away from the back of her neck, I let my breath brush against her ear.

My head spun in a whirlwind of feelings, and I allowed myself to get lost in them.

In her.

I could sense that her eyes followed the movement of my strong arms as they came around her body. Skimming the sides of her ribs, I placed my hands on the railing in front of her, caging her against my torso.

My scent.

My thoughts.

My words.

My emotions.

They all seemed to intertwine with one another, pushing and pulling like a game of tug-of-war.

I heard her take a deep breath, knowing she was happy. In the grand scheme of things, this was a very simple gesture, but to Livvy, this meant everything, and I hadn't gotten to the biggest surprise yet. It was one of the traits I loved the most about her. She wasn't like other girls. It was the simple stuff that truly made her smile.

For me, the hardest part of her moving was that I wouldn't be there to experience another monumental independent moment in her life. It was the hardest pill to swallow, but I couldn't hold her back from experiencing new things without me.

However, I didn't have to fucking like it either.

My role in her life was to be there for her when she needed me, and this situation wasn't any different. Kissing her neck, I let my lip linger momentarily before grabbing her hand and leading her deeper into the forest. It didn't take long to step into the surprise I had waiting for her.

The moment she saw the jars of ladybugs, she loudly gasped.

In her ear, I rasped, "I thought we could free them."

"I can't believe you did this."

She opened the first jar to set a few of them free. Without her noticing, I started to film her with my phone. Wanting to record this memory so that I could watch it whenever I wanted. She looked like a Disney princess, spinning around as she freed all the ladybugs. Loving every second of it.

She thanked me during the entire drive to the indoor amusement park, and when we pulled into the parking lot, she climbed in my lap and showed me how thankful she truly was by riding my cock.

Livvy was as competitive as they come. After I beat her at every single game, she claimed I was cheating and didn't want to play with me anymore, so I took her on the Ferris wheel and reminded her that she wanted to play with me just fine instead.

"Wow... you really went all out for our first date," she coaxed, sitting in front of me at the restaurant for dinner.

"It's not over." I smiled, setting a wrapped box in the center of us on the table.

"What is that?"

"Open it and find out."

She picked it up. "But you wrapped it so nicely."

"I do what I can."

"Why am I getting a present?"

"In case we can't be together on your birthday."

She sadly smiled. "Right..." Shaking it off, she opened it. "Ethan..."

It was a gold necklace with a key hanging off it.
We locked eyes.
"Why a key?"
I didn't hesitate to reply...
"Because you own my heart."

Chapter Eleven
ETHAN

Summer was almost over.

Livvy would be leaving to move to California soon. Two weeks to be exact. I had no fucking clue where we went from here. We only briefly discussed it that one time when she asked me what we were to each other. Now that her moving day was quickly approaching, it felt like a ticking time bomb waiting to explode.

How do we go back to just being best friends after this summer?

It changed everything. Looking back on it now, I began to feel like Livvy regretted how far we'd taken things. For the past few days, she had begun to pull away from me.

She was quiet.

Inattentive and unresponsive.

Half the time, she seemed as if she was lost in her own little world.

At the end of the day, all that truly mattered to me was our friendship. I had said that since day one before we started any of this on prom night.

As much as I hated to admit it, maybe the distance would be good for us. I couldn't help but think about what her old man asked of me the same night I claimed his daughter's virginity. I didn't consider the consequences of us sleeping together, and now, for the life of me, I couldn't think about them. Especially how right it felt being with her all this time.

Except now she wasn't returning my calls.

Or answering my texts.

It was like she was trying to disappear.

This was the longest we'd ever gone without speaking, so when she texted me that morning, wanting to meet at our waterhole, I jumped in my truck and headed that way with nothing but uncertainty and anxiety. It was almost crippling how much fear I felt for the future and what she'd say to me. I never felt like this before, and I wouldn't wish it on my worst enemy.

I parked my truck and found her sitting on her swing. Even with the distance between us, I could see she was crying as I made my way over to her.

"Fuck," I muttered under my breath.

This couldn't be good. Livvy didn't cry. She hated it, but she was still so beautiful, so breathtakingly beautiful. Her hair was down and flowing through the light breeze, it was the only part of her that moved with ease. She was wearing a white dress which was my favorite color on her, and I wondered if she did that for me.

I could visibly tell she was uncomfortable in her own skin. I walked slower the closer I approached her. As soon as I stood beside her, she shut her eyes like it pained her to be near me. The warmth that usually radiated off her was missing.

She was cold.

Detached.

It was hard for me to swallow for a few seconds before she opened them again to look out toward the water. She suddenly leaned her head on my stomach, and I held back the desire to wrap my arm around her, but then she did it herself.

I felt her take three deep, steady breaths before she somewhat relaxed against me. We stayed in complete silence for the rest of the afternoon, watching the world revolve around us as if we were the only two people in it. The bright colors of the sky started giving way to nightfall, blending perfectly into deep oranges to fire reds. Sunsets in Charleston were always a sight to behold. No matter where you were.

I was the first to break the silence. "Livvy, are you going to tell me what's wrong?"

Instead of replying, she pulled me down onto the seat, shifting to straddle my waist and sit on my lap.

"What are you—"

She placed her finger on my lips. "Shhh..."

I cocked my head to the side, confused.

"Shhh..." she repeated, looking intently into my eyes, searching for something in my stare I couldn't quite place.

Using her finger that was already on my lips, she gently brushed it back and forth against my mouth. Parting them to rub along the inside where she could feel my breath. I didn't stop her. I let her do what she wanted, what she needed, in hopes of seeing my girl again.

Slowly, she slid her finger along the edge of my face, tracing my jawbone from one side to the other. Moving to my cheeks, then the bridge of my nose up to my forehead. She was just touching ever so softly along my skin. Our eyes stayed connected the entire time. She licked her lips as she swiped her finger to my chin and neck, stopping to caress the front of my throat with her thumb.

As she made her way down to my chest, she broke eye contact to focus on my heart before tracing her fingers along it, hardly touching me at all. When she firmly placed the palm of her right hand against my heart, I saw a subtle smile appear on her face.

It was quick, but it was there.

She joined our left hands and brought them up to her heart, pressing her fingers on the backside of my hand to hold it in place. It beat a mile a minute, nothing compared to my steady beat. I waited for her next move, feeling her rapid heartbeat pounding against my hand as she leaned in to kiss me.

Slow.

Gentle.

She took her time to explore my mouth.

I cherished every second before I felt her unbuckle my jeans.

"Livvy—"

She pulled out my cock, causing me to groan.

As if reading my mind, she sensed my hesitation, whispering, "Just be with me. Please..." So much sadness laced her voice.

Despair.

Agony.

What's going on?

I reluctantly nodded with an immense amount of emotions coursing through my body that I couldn't find the words to speak.

Her stare melted as she raised her dress over her head and was left wearing only her panties, but those were quickly gone as well. I could feel her thoughts raging a war in her mind when she wrapped her legs around my waist.

"Where's my girl?" I rasped into her ear. "Where's my Livvy?"

"I'm right here."

With her hands framing my face, she kissed me. "I want you," she moaned.

This moment didn't feel like it did every time before this.

"Livvy," I breathed against her mouth. "Talk to me."

Her tiny, delicate hand stroked my dick up and down. Her grip barely closed around my shaft, making my balls ache.

Every blush of her face.

Every moan from her lips.

Had my cock throbbing in pain, dying to be inside her.

In one swift movement, she eased her way down my dick. Inch by inch, a little more each time until her mouth parted and her eyes shut tightly. I filled her to the tilt.

Our connection.

Our friendship.

Our love.

Ethan.

Livvy.

One.

With a hard, strong hold, I gripped her hips, rocking her back and forth on my cock.

Over and over again.

She locked her arms around my neck, and we fervently kissed as she rode me there on her swing, where we shut out the whole world.

It was just the two of us.

And I never wanted to leave.

"You're so fucking beautiful with my cock inside you."

My other hand roughly dug into her hip bone, helping her ride me. I could feel her pussy tighten, gripping my cock like a fucking vise. Vaguely feeling her shiver.

I growled, "Fuck... you feel good." Thrusting my hips upward, I roughly gripped her hips again.

Our mouths parted.

Breathless.

Riding the high, waiting to fall over the edge together.

I slid my tongue into her mouth when I felt her pussy throb, pulsating long and tight.

"There's my girl," I groaned, needing her to hear it.

Her eyes immediately rimmed with fresh tears, and I kissed them all away as they slid down her cheeks.

"What's wrong?" I questioned, desperately trying to read her expression and searching her face for an answer I couldn't find.

I was always so in tune with her gaze, and at that moment, they were indescribable, but I didn't care because I was inside her. We were together, and I held on to her for as long as I could. Livvy would never fully understand what she meant to me.

Maybe that was my fault.

Maybe I should have said it to her more.

Maybe it would have stopped what happened in the days to follow and in the years to come.

Maybe...

Maybe...

Maybe...

Something took over me. This primal urge wreaked havoc in the agonizing rhythm of how we were coming. Clinging onto every sensation of our skin-on-skin contact until she came so hard, squeezing my cock and taking me right along with her. I shook with my release and passionately claimed her mouth again. She returned every ounce of everything I was giving her while my lock and key necklace shined bright against her skin.

There was no holding back.

No fighting it.

We were making love and I knew right then and there—nothing would ever compare to her.

To us.

I'd spend the next decade trying to fill this void, this hole, this feeling she left inside me. Never realizing it was useless. I thought I could eventually fuck her out of my heart, but she owned it, and I willingly gave it to her. Not once did I ask for it back.

"My girl," I groaned between kissing. Needing to get to the bottom of her despair, I begged, "Please tell me what's wrong?"

"Ethan…" She bowed her head. "I'm sorry… I'm so sorry…"

My heart drummed.

My stomach dropped.

My whole world shattered in the blink of an eye.

Is she saying goodbye?

Tears streamed down her gorgeous face. One right after the other. There was no controlling them.

"Livvy… you're scaring me."

"I'm late…" she whispered so low I barely heard her.

My eyebrows pinched together because I'm still not understanding what that meant.

"Late for what?"

Five words had the power to break us before we had a chance to explore what could have been. I thought sex might change our friendship, and in the end, I was right.

Because all in one breath, she cried…

"I'm late for my period."

Chapter Twelve

LIVVY

His eyes widened, and his face immediately paled.

"I know," I stated, feeling the weight of my confession.

"How late?"

"Ten days."

Just hearing me say it out loud for the first time was enough to destroy me all at once.

I broke down.

Bawling.

Shaking.

Utterly defensive.

"I can't do this," I wept, fervently shaking my head while still sitting on his lap. "I'm only eighteen. You're only eighteen. We can't be parents. I can barely take care of myself, and what about college? I can't have a baby in college. My dad is going to kill me, Ethan. He's going to fucking kill me."

"It's okay." He pulled me into the tightest hug. "You're okay."

I shoved him away and jumped off his lap to grab my dress and threw it on. This wasn't what I wanted to hear. Although I didn't even know what I wanted to hear. I was so confused. My mind raced with thoughts about the future. Question after question tore through my mind with no end in sight.

I couldn't breathe.

I felt like I couldn't breathe.

Simply reacting to his composed demeanor, I snapped, "I'm far from okay, Ethan!"

He raised his hands in a surrendering gesture. "We'll figure it out."

"How are you not freaking out?"

Ignoring my question, he asked, "Did you take a test?"

I winced, shaking my head again. "I was too scared of what it would say."

He hesitantly nodded. "That's the first thing we need to do."

"But what if—"

"Livvy, we'll cross that bridge when we get there. First, we need to make sure you're not just late because you've been stressing out about moving. It could be from that."

"But what if it isn't?"

He shrugged. "Then it isn't."

"That's all you have to say?"

"For now, yes."

Unable to control my reckless emotions, I bit, "How could we let this happen? How, Ethan?! I'm on the pill! I take it at the same time every day like fucking clockwork. This can't be happening. It just can't! This has to be a bad dream! We can't be parents!"

I was at my wit's end. The thread I was hanging onto ripped in half and I couldn't for the life of me find any comfort in what he was saying. If anything, it just further pissed me off.

Spitting fire, I roared, "This isn't happening to you!" I sternly pointed at myself. "This is happening to me! It's my body! I'm the one who's going to have to go through everything."

He abruptly stood, buckling his shorts.

"It's so easy for the guy! This changes my entire life, Ethan! Every last second of it!"

I knew I was being irrational, but I couldn't help it. This didn't feel like his problem. It only felt like mine, and I couldn't see past that.

"You need to calm down. We don't even know if you're pregnant yet. This could be—"

"We should have never had sex to begin with! How did we let it get this far? We were reckless to think we could handle something like this."

I could see it in his eyes, he knew I was right. We didn't stop to think about the consequences of entering a sexual friendship. I don't think we thought about anything other than screwing each other's brains out.

Except this was Ethan Carter.

He wasn't just a random boy.

A random fuck.

This was my best friend.

He was my best friend.

I yanked my hair back, wanting to rip it out of my head. "Ugh! Fuck!"

He reached for me in an understanding gesture of what I was saying. "Livvy."

I stepped back. "Please don't touch me right now. All I keep thinking is that I'm eighteen years old and I'm still a kid. How on earth can I take care of one if I'm still one myself? We both are."

"Exactly, you're not alone in this. I know it may feel like that right now, but if you are pregnant, we'll figure it out together. I'm not going anywhere. We need to take a test."

"But what if I am?"

"But what if you aren't?"

"But what if I am?" I insisted. "I'm never late. Ever." My head felt like it was going to explode. "Everything is happening so fast, Ethan. We aren't together. I'm not your girlfriend, and you're not my boyfriend. We're not in a relationship, and now we may have messed up both our lives."

"You're just scared, Livvy, and you're freaking out."

"How are you not? This would mess up your entire future."

"I'd make it work."

"Let me remind you, you're on a full-ride scholarship, Ethan. If you don't keep your GPA up, then guess what? You lose it. You don't have time for a baby, let alone a job to—"

"Why don't you let me worry about that, alright?"

"I can't believe you."

He shrugged. "A baby's always a blessing. Regardless of how much of an inconvenience it could be."

"Great, so I guess that makes me the selfish bitch because I'm thinking about our futures."

"Don't put words in my mouth."

I sighed deeply, trying to gather my emotions for a second. "I'm sorry I can't see past how much this would mess up our futures."

He stepped toward me, and to my surprise, I didn't back away from him this time. Since I didn't, he quickly reached over and caressed my cheek with the back of his fingers.

"The only thing we can do right now is take a test and go from there, but if you are, that's my baby too, and don't you ever fucking forget that. We're in this together. Do you understand me?"

I nodded, throwing my arms around his neck, and he instantly hugged me back.

"No matter what, I love you, Livvy," he murmured in my ear. "And don't you ever fucking forget that either."

I wouldn't.

I couldn't.

Meaning it from the bottom of my heart, I expressed, "I love you too."

I frantically hung onto him for dear life.

ETHAN

I thought five words would change the rest of our lives, but I was wrong.

It was one.

Pregnant.

Bright.

Bold.

Clear as day to read.

I barely had time to register the results before Livvy crumpled to the ground on my bathroom floor. I immediately pulled her into my arms, and her face tucked into the crook of my neck.

She instantly broke down.

She cried so hard her body was shaking.

I couldn't control the tsunami of feelings that coursed through her body. I simply held her as tight as I could as if I was going to hold her together.

"It's okay... I promise it will be okay," I repeated, hoping she'd listen to me.

Believe in me.

In us.

Nothing I could say or do made her feel at ease, so I just let her cry in my arms. We stayed there like that for hours until I picked her up off the floor and carried her to my bed, where I spent the rest of the night just comforting her the only way I knew how.

Suddenly, she pulled away from me and abruptly stood.

"Livvy—"

"I gotta go." She snapped around, but she wasn't fast enough. I jumped off my bed, and I was in her face before she took a step.

Grabbing her face between my hands, I reminded her, "It's going to be okay. Do you hear me?"

She didn't say a word.

Her gaze looked lifeless.

Almost like she was numb or in shock.

"I'll make an appointment with the doctor. Don't worry about anything. I'll handle it for us."

Again, silence.

"Livvy, I need to hear you say you know that I'm not going anywhere."

Nothing.

Not one damn thing.

I preferred her frightened than like this. It was so out of character for her, which terrified me more than anything.

Slowly, I kissed her lips, and for the first time, she didn't respond to my touch. As much as I tried, I couldn't get through to her. She tuned me out. Instead, I reluctantly let her go, watching her leave.

I feared for the worst.

Not that she was pregnant, but that...

We may have ruined our friendship.

Chapter Thirteen

LIVVY

I leaned back against the headrest in the passenger seat of Ethan's truck. I hadn't seen or spoken to him for the past week despite how often he reached out, but he left me alone for the most part. I think he needed as much space as I did.

One minute, we're best friends.

The next, we're pregnant.

Everything was happening so fast, and I was barely surviving it. Nobody knew what was happening. I couldn't bring myself to tell my parents. As far as they knew, I was moving next week, and my mom started packing for me last night.

She didn't give me a hard time. Almost like she knew I was going through something. My guess would be that she thought it was just about Ethan and moving away from him. I let her assume whatever she wanted, too worried about how she'd react to the disaster that my life unexpectedly turned into. I did my best to act like I wasn't internally flipping out as I watched her effortlessly move around my room like my life wasn't falling apart.

That morning, everything came to a head. It took a week for the OB-GYN to see us, and I couldn't have been more grateful to Ethan for handling everything. The last thing I wanted to do was argue with him again. I didn't have the energy for it. Too much had happened, and I already told him how I felt. He was fully aware of how much this was tearing me up, and nothing he could say or do would take that away.

"Livvy," Ethan announced, making me realize he wasn't driving anymore, and we were parked in the lot of the doctor's office.

Still not looking at him, I spoke the truth, "I can't do this. How are we going do this?"

He grabbed my hand, causing me to peer over at him.

"Let's see what the doctor says before we head down this road, alright?"

"How are you still so calm?" I muttered above a whisper until I finally got a good look at him.

He appeared as exhausted as I felt. It looked like he hadn't slept since we found out, making me feel horrible that I wasn't there for my best friend.

"Ethan, I'm sorry. I know this affects you too, and I truly appreciate you staying calm. I don't think I could've handled both of us losing our shit."

"I'm the one who should be apologizing. I should have been there for you this past week, but I—"

"I know." I nodded in reassurance. "How did we let this come between our friendship? We swore we wouldn't let anything affect that, and now look at us, we're barely on speaking terms."

"I know," he murmured. "But we're going to be okay, I promise."

I faintly smiled. "Whatever happens, Ethan. I'm glad it happened with you."

"Me too, Livvy."

Once we were inside the office, it didn't take long for my name to be called and for me to be sitting on the examination table. Ethan sat in the empty chair in the corner of the room with his elbows on his knees, staring at the floor. For some reason, seeing him that way broke my heart in ways I hadn't expected. I didn't know which one was worse, seeing him calm or seeing him like this.

Thank God all they had to do was draw my blood to confirm what we already knew. We both sat there, lost in the turmoil of a future we hadn't predicted. Not for one second.

When there was a loud knock on the door, I jumped out of my skin, completely unprepared for what happened next. Moments later, Dr. Taylor stepped inside, closing the door behind her.

"Hello," she greeted, looking at my chart in her hands. "I'm Dr. Taylor." She glanced up. "You must be Elizabeth?"

"Yes."

She smiled. "Nice to meet you."

I pointed at Ethan. "That's Ethan. He's, ummm... my best friend."

His stare locked with mine.

"How nice of him to come here with you. I don't get to see a lot of that." She paused, looking at my chart one last time before she added, "Well then, my nurse caught me up on everything, and I have your blood results for your pregnancy test in my hand."

I nodded, feeling as if I would pass the hell out.

"Would you like me to confirm your results?"

"Your blood shows that you're..."

This was the moment of truth.

Three.

Two.

One.

"Not pregnant."

"What?" I exclaimed, caught off guard. "The pregnancy test I took said I was."

"Sometimes false positives can happen, but blood doesn't lie. You're not pregnant, Elizabeth."

The immediate relief was like a shot of adrenaline through my veins.

"I see in your chart that you're on the pill, correct?"

"Yes."

"Okay, great. I don't think I need to tell you how important it is to make sure you're taking it on time and not skipping days? Especially if you're sexually active."

"Yes, of course. I am."

"That's great to hear." She stood. "We also have other forms of contraceptives, but if you'd prefer to stay on the pill, it doesn't hurt to use a condom as well."

"Right, that's probably smart."

"You're still very young, and until you're ready to have a baby, it's better to be safe than sorry."

"Yes, Dr. Taylor. Thank you for the advice."

"No problem. Are there any other questions you have for me?"

"No, I'm good, thank you."

"It was nice meeting you, Elizabeth." She glanced back and forth between us. "You two take care."

I wish I could tell you that this instantly fixed everything between us, but I'd be lying. Neither one of us spoke on the drive back to my house. After Ethan stopped his truck at the end of my driveway, I knew he wasn't coming inside, and I didn't know why I expected him to.

Especially with everything we just went through.

Stating the obvious, I uttered, "I leave next week."

He nodded, staring out in front of him.

"Are we okay?"

He eyed me. "Of course."

The sudden silence was deafening.

I had no clue what to say or even how to say it. Where to begin, how to end. Although, the relief was there for not being pregnant. A whole other emotion showed up and that was terror of us not being able to get back to where we were prior to having sex.

I didn't want to lose him.

I couldn't.

I wouldn't survive it.

As if reading my mind, he asked, "Do you want me to help you pack?"

"Yeah, if you want to."

He faintly smiled, parking his truck in my driveway.

We spent the next few hours packing up my room until my mom walked in.

"Aw," she professed with her hand over her heart. "This might be the last time you're in this room together for a while."

Ethan greeted, "Hello, Mrs. Collins."

"Aren't you sweet to help Elizabeth pack. She's going to miss you so much."

"Mom..."

"I know, I know. You don't want me to fuss, but as your mother, I'm allowed to feel emotional right now. My baby girl is moving away for college. I'm so beyond proud of you, but that doesn't mean I'm not sad you're leaving."

"You can blame your husband for that," I stated, not holding back.

She gave me a sympathetic smile, sitting on the edge of my bed while I sat on the floor packing my bookshelves with Ethan beside me.

"Sweetheart, I know it feels that way, but we just want what's best for you."

"By taking me away from everything I know?"

"This is the perfect time for you to explore your independence. You two have been inseparable for as long as I can remember. I can't believe how fast time has flown by. It feels like you two were running around the house playing hide-and-go-seek just yesterday." She paused, allowing her words to sink in.

"I know you're upset with your father, but trust me when I say he's going to miss you like crazy. We both are. Except we know this is what you two need. You two will always be best friends. Distance isn't going to change that. Plus, you'll be visiting often, and I'm sure Ethan will be visiting you too. It's a great opportunity for you two to appreciate how important you are to each other."

Is she right?

"Ethan, you know I adore you, and you've always been there for my baby girl. I couldn't have asked for a better best friend for my daughter. I count my blessings every day that she has you in her life. You've been nothing but a positive influence, and the way you've loved her wholeheartedly isn't something I've ever overlooked. You're lucky to have one another." She smirked. "I promise. This will only strengthen your friendship, and one day, who knows, maybe it'll turn into something else, but you'll never find out until you both find yourselves. Do you understand what I'm saying?"

As much as I hated to admit it, she was right. After she left to answer the call from my dad—his ears must have been ringing—Ethan turned to face me.

"She's right."

I lightly gasped.

"I think this last week or two has proved how right she is."

"You don't mean that."

"I do, and you know it too. You're just too stubborn to admit it, so I'll do it for us both."

"What are you saying?"

"I'm saying we'll forever be best friends, and nothing will change that, but if this pregnancy scare proved anything, it's how much we're not ready to be anything other than that."

"Are you saying you regret us having sex?"

He shrugged. "I'm not sure. All I know is that I never want sex to come between us again. You're too important to me."

"But—"

"You were right, Livvy. I'm not your boyfriend. You're not my girlfriend. We're not in a relationship. We never were. I want you to go to college and not think about what happened between us this summer. I want to go back to what mattered the most, which was our friendship. I can't lose you. I won't."

"Yeah..." That was all I could reply.

"I'll always be here for you, and I know you'll be there for me too. Nothing can change that. It doesn't matter how many miles are between us. You're part of me, like I'm part of you."

Needing him to hear it, I coaxed, "I love you, Ethan."

He smiled. "You still my girl?"

I didn't waver in speaking with conviction...

"Always."

Chapter Fourteen

ETHAN

"*Ethan...*"

I groaned, shaking my head. Stirring awake beneath my white tangled sheets as I faintly felt someone's lips laying soft kisses down the side of my neck.

"*Ethan, I'm sorry. I'm so sorry.*"

My eyes fluttered, trying to wake up, but my body wouldn't allow it, and sleep won out. I was beyond exhausted from not sleeping over the last two weeks, and when my head hit the pillow that night, I was out like a light.

Dreaming only about Livvy.

She was leaving tomorrow.

Moving away.

I had helped her pack all week, and even in my deep slumber, I could still smell her intoxicating honey scent and feel her smooth lips along my heated skin.

"*Ethan, wake up...*"

"Mm-hmm," I hummed, feeling her lips trail toward my stomach.

Kiss by kiss.

Peck by peck.

Inch by inch.

Until she reached my happy trail, making my cock twitch at the heady feel of her mouth so close to my dick. I fisted my sheets, wanting, needing her lips wrapped around my cock.

I felt her delicate fingers tug the waistband of my gym shorts down, whispering, *"Please, just be with me."*

My breathing hitched, and my eyes snapped open, big and wide as I came face-to-face with the last person I expected to see hovering above me.

Livvy.

There was no way I was still dreaming, but if this happened to be a dream within a dream, then I never wanted to wake up. At that moment, the world stopped spinning, stopped moving, and time just stood still for us. Even with the dim lighting of the moon, I could see her beautiful face in front of me.

She looked stunning and tortured all at once.

I couldn't form words.

I couldn't think.

Not when she was looking at me like that.

She stared into my eyes, searching for something in my gaze. As if she was looking for some recognition of who I was or maybe traces of who she was when she was with me.

"Livvy..." I rasped, my voice laced thick with uncertainty and concern. "What are you doing here?"

"My flight is in the morning."

"I know."

"I couldn't leave without erasing the last few weeks of our friendship."

I cocked my head to the side, and my eyebrows pinched together.

"I just want to be with you one last time."

"Livvy, we just went through—"

"I know. Trust me, I'm fully aware, but I don't want our last memory of making love to be on a swing before I told you I was late for my period. We can't end like that, Ethan. I refuse to end like that."

"It would be so reckless if we—"

She showed me a condom. "And I just finished my period. It'd be nearly impossible for that to happen."

I thought about it for a second. She was right.

"I know you don't want to end the way we did either. I know this won't change anything between us, but I need closure, so I can at least remember our last time being about us and not the desperation of trying to escape. Please... just be with me."

I didn't know what to say. I barely knew how to feel.

"I just need a better goodbye before I go. It feels like an elephant has been in my room with us all week, and I know it's because of how things ended. I know this will help both of us move on. At least it will for me. You're forever my best friend, but I'm losing my lover, and I didn't even get a chance to say goodbye to him. We owe each other that. Don't you think?"

I narrowed my gaze. "Livvy—"

"Shhh..." She leaned forward, placing her lips close to mine. "Stop thinking. All we have is right now. Just. Right. Now." Her eyes watered, fighting back the tears. "Please..."

Her pleading tone shook me to my core as a single tear slid down her beautiful face. The next thing I knew, she kissed me, beckoning me to do the same.

"Livv—"

"Shhh..." she coaxed against my mouth. "All we have is right now," she repeated.

My mind battled my heart, raging a war I never had a chance of winning. Her loneliness ate me alive, swallowing me whole. I decided to do the only thing I could for her and for me. I sought refuge in the right now, which was good enough for me.

So I did what I had to do, what felt right and so fucking true.

I kissed her back with my heart breaking, piece by piece, crumbling to the ground as I made up for the last three weeks that felt as if I couldn't breathe.

For each tear.

Each regret.

Each moment we needed one another but weren't there for each other.

For the past where we became best friends and the present where we became lovers, down to the future we so desperately wanted together, but there would forever be an endless number of obstacles in our way.

We kissed.

And kissed.

And kissed some more...

We kissed until none of that fucking mattered until it felt like we were simply breathing for one another. Until all that was finally left...

Was us.

Ethan and Livvy.

The way it was always meant to be, no matter what. Deep down in my stomach, I knew this wouldn't change anything between us. Our lives were on two different journeys.

Instead of dwelling on that, I grabbed the back of her neck, bringing her closer to me as if she wasn't already close enough. Sitting up, I flipped our bodies over so I was now lying on top of her, yearning to feel her beneath me.

Resting my arms by the sides of her face, I started lowering my frame onto her petite, trembling body. Cherishing every second our lips moved against one another. Our mouths starved for the affection, ached for the warmth, and longed to lose ourselves.

Reaching for the hem of her dress, I slid it off her body, leaving her in nothing but her panties and distress.

So exposed.

So vulnerable.

So fucking afflicted.

With a predatory regard, I devoured every inch of her bare skin, from her rosy-colored nipples to her perky, supple tits, down to her narrow, slender waist, and her luscious ass and thighs before I slipped off her panties and crawled up her body. Spreading her legs for me, I lay between them, kissing her all over again.

From her lips, her cheeks, to the tip of her nose, and down to the sides of her neck. Kissing, licking, caressing my way toward her nipples while my fingers coasted along her smooth, silky skin, trailing all over her naked body.

The addictive sounds she made.

The way her body kept shuddering beneath mine.

The smell of her arousal.

It had me losing my mind.

I flicked, sucked, slightly bit her nipples, driving her wild with need. Working my way toward where I wanted to be the most, I peered up at her through the slits of my eyes.

With a sly grin, I pulled down my gym shorts, freeing my hard, thick cock. Her eyes widened while I jerked it in my hand. Never once taking my eyes off hers as I sparingly skimmed my lips over her bare heat.

I watched her swallow hard, her chest rising and falling, waiting, eager, ready...

Grinning, I nudged my nose along her folds, faintly blowing the entire time. Gradually, lightly, I ran the tip of my tongue over her clit, hearing her breathe, heavy and deep.

"Is this what you came for?"

"Please," she begged in a breathless tone.

Our eyes connected, and I let go of my cock and gripped her thighs. Locking them in place at the sides of my face, I put her exactly where I wanted her. She rocked her hips, arching her back and making my cock twitch for what felt like the hundredth time.

As soon as I sucked her clit into my mouth, she moaned as I savored her taste and the feel of her while her legs tightened around me. Sliding my finger into her tight little hole, I gently, purposely finger-fucked her G-spot, getting her nice and ready to take my cock.

I devoured her, lustfully lapping up and down, side to side.

So wet.

She tasted so good.

Her pussy throbbed.

Her body shook.

"Ethan," she panted, over and over as she came in my mouth, again and again.

"Ethan, please..." she begged for mercy, but I didn't stop. I couldn't.

She consumed me.

From my mind to my soul, to my fucking cock.

How do I let her go?

After I finally made her mine.

"Ethan... I can't... I can't come... any... more..."

"One more, give me one more."

And she did. But even that wasn't enough for me. I was like a man possessed, licking her fucking clean. Thrusting my tongue into her opening, I was unable to get enough of her.

I craved it all.

Every last drop of her.

I relentlessly kissed her overly stimulated clit one last time, causing her to shudder again before I crawled my way back up to her lips. I kissed her as if my life depended on it, making her taste herself. Needing her to realize that no other man would ever be able to claim her like this.

She was mine.

She'd always be mine.

Growling into her mouth, I battled new demons.

I imagined another man's mouth on her.

Another man's hands.

Another man's cock.

"Livvy." I set my forehead against hers, gazing into her eyes. "I can't do this. It's going to make it harder."

"Please..." she urged in the same yearning tone, with the same desperate look in her eyes.

There wasn't a chance in hell I could say no to her.

I belonged to her.

She owned me.

Every last part of me was hers.

Taking a deep breath, I peered deep into her eyes, searching for my girl. She kissed me, lifting her hips, silently demanding me to keep going. When I didn't move fast enough, she reached for my dick and wrapped her hand around my shaft, causing my breath to hitch against her lips and my dick to jerk in her grasp. There was no hesitation on her part, rolling the condom down the shaft of my cock.

"Stop thinking, Ethan, and just be with me."

My plaguing thoughts refused to let me go. I tried like hell to get lost in the sensation by taking a moment once I was fully inside her, but it was no use.

She kissed me again. "I feel it all too." Gradually rotating her hips, she adjusted to the size of my dick.

She was so tight.

So warm.

So perfect.

"Promise me that no matter what happens or who comes along, you'll always remember that you were mine first?"

Tears escaped her eyes, sliding down the sides of her face. She nodded, moaning, "I promise."

We were two bodies swimming in a sea of emotions, of mistakes and regrets, of the pain of tomorrow and every day after that.

She gasped the second she felt my fingers rubbing against her clit. I picked up my pace, driving her further and further to the edge, about to fall over.

"Ethan... right there."

"Where, baby, here?"

"Oh God... yes... right there..." I claimed her lips, muffling her screams as she came all down my shaft.

Squeezing the fuck out of my cock.

Harder.

Faster.

Deeper.

"Come on my cock, Livvy. Yeah, just like that."

Her sweet pussy sucked my dick dry. I came so hard, I saw stars. My body shuddered right along with hers. Both of us went over the edge together, where I could barely see straight. Our pleasure didn't last nearly long enough until the pain took over. Feeling her silently break down, her body trembled in my arms with tears cascading down her gorgeous face. Falling onto the sheets we just made love on.

We stayed like that for I don't know how long, in our haven that may have turned into our hell. It felt as if an eternity had passed between us, yet it still wasn't enough time with her.

Never enough time.

Kissing all over her face again, I slowly, unwillingly, pulled out of her, causing her to wince from my loss. I kissed the tip of her nose and stood, going straight into the bathroom. I needed a minute to myself for what I wasn't prepared for. My emotions held me hostage while I cleaned myself up. I was failing miserably at trying to keep my shit together.

I took a deep breath, making my way back into the room. She was in the same position I left her, staring up at the ceiling. Lost in her own thoughts with my white sheet wrapped around her naked torso. Before she knew what I was doing, I grabbed her and laid her on top of me.

She peered up at me with fresh tears in her eyes, biting her bottom lip. Overwhelmed and disheveled. I closed my eyes. I had to. I was unable to look at her any longer even though she had always been my favorite thing to look at. The next thing I knew, she kissed all over my face, wrapping her arms and legs around me, seeking the comfort she needed in my embrace.

I kissed her, softly pecking her lips, taking my time with each stroke of my tongue as it tangled with hers.

I tasted her tears.

Once I opened my eyes, I saw every sentiment I felt through her gaze. She allowed me to see her again. Her walls were down, and her flag was up.

She surrendered.

To me.

To us.

More tears slid down her tortured face, and I kissed those away as well.

"I said this from the very beginning at prom night. No matter what happened between us, it doesn't change that we're forever best friends. I won't lose you, Livvy. At least not like that."

Elizabeth Collins was my beginning and now the time had come for our ending. I just didn't know what hurt more, the fact that this was our conclusion...

Or the fact that she'd be leaving tomorrow.

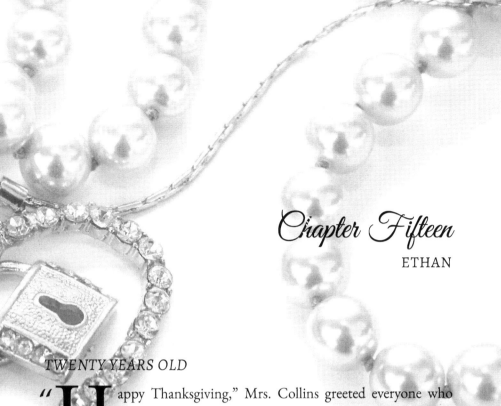

Chapter Fifteen

ETHAN

TWENTY YEARS OLD

"Happy Thanksgiving," Mrs. Collins greeted everyone who walked through their door.

She wanted to surprise Livvy that she invited me to dinner at their home for the holiday. This wasn't the first time I'd spend Thanksgiving at the Collins estate, and I was sure it wouldn't be the last. She said she wanted to have everyone there, and by everyone, I mean everyone. Their house was packed with people, and Livvy's plane landed an hour ago.

She thought I'd be in Kansas, where my uncle moved for his job, and that was my initial plan until her mother called me a few days ago and begged me to join them. I appreciated the invitation. The last time I saw Livvy was during the summer. I stayed at her place for a week, and our friendship returned to what it always was.

We saw each other a few times a year, but we talked a couple of times a week and texted every day about something. We were both busy with school, and I didn't have time for much else. I was in the process of developing a social media app that no one knew about. Not even Livvy. It was still a work in progress. I was determined to create it, and nothing would stop me until I did.

"Hello, Ethan," Livvy's dad announced, coming up behind me as I stood outside by their Olympic-size pool.

"Hello, Mr. Collins, how are you?"

"I'll have my whole family under one roof soon. I couldn't be better."

I smiled, nodding.

"My wife tells me that Livvy doesn't know you're in town, and that you'll be here tonight."

"Yeah, Mrs. Collins wanted to keep it a surprise for her."

"I'm sure Livvy will love that."

I smiled again.

"You know, Ethan. I never got to thank you for helping us with talking Livvy into attending Stanford."

"You don't need to thank me. I didn't do anything."

He gripped my shoulder, affirming, "You let her go, and that's what she needed." With a gentle squeeze, he nodded for us to walk into the foyer at the same time as the front door opened, and Livvy stepped in.

Her eyes widened as soon as she saw me standing in front of her.

"Surprise," I exclaimed, taking her in.

Only then did I notice that she cut her long, red hair. It no longer lay down her back. It was the shortest I'd ever seen it, and it was a little above her shoulders, framing her petite face.

"You cut your hair?" I asked, surprised.

She shyly smiled. "I did."

"You look stunn—"

"Liv, baby, you almost left your cell phone in the Uber."

My gaze abruptly shifted to the man walking in behind her with her phone in his hand.

He wrapped his arm around her waist, tugging her toward him to kiss her cheek. "You'd be lost without me."

My eyebrows raised, caught off guard was an understatement.

She locked eyes with me and introduced him, "Ethan, this is Beau."

He instantly extended out his hand for me to shake. "Ethan, it's nice to finally meet you. I've heard so much about you."

Eyeing him up and down, I scoffed out, "That's nice, considering I haven't heard a damn thing about you."

"Ethan," Livvy reprimanded in a stern tone before her dad interrupted us.

"My baby girl," Mr. Collins celebrated, pulling her into a tight hug. *Who the fuck is Beau?*

Her mother quickly followed, hugging her too. "Sweetheart, you cut your hair. I love it." Glancing over at me, she added, "Did you see our surprise?"

Livvy cautiously replied, "I did."

Mrs. Collins's stare moved to Beau. "Who's this?"

"Now I know where Livvy gets her beauty from." He shook her hand. "I'm Beau. Livvy's boyfriend."

I jerked back like he'd punch me in the stomach.

"Oh!" Mrs. Collins smiled. "I didn't know Livvy had a boyfriend."

I chimed in, "That makes two of us."

Livvy nervously chuckled. "I was going to introduce you to him tonight, Mom."

"I guess you came home with your own surprise," Mrs. Collins remarked. "Well, Beau. Welcome to our home. I'm Livvy's mother, and this is her father."

Her parents started talking to him, and I didn't hear a word they said. I couldn't stop staring at how close Beau was to Livvy. How he still had his hand on the swell of her back and rubbed up and down with every word they said. Livvy stayed involved in their conversation and I had to step away from them.

I had no right to be upset, but there it was.

Bright.

Red.

Anger.

The truth was, it wasn't just the rage I felt, it was jealousy that ate me fucking alive. The night went on with its normal festivities, and pretty boy Beau didn't leave Livvy's side the entire time.

Everything stopped.

Everything.

I swear to God my heart stopped beating in my chest, only for a second, and then a surge of panic flooded my body, my mind, and my soul at precisely the moment my heart began beating again.

Loud and hard.

Once we were sitting at the table, eating dinner, Beau lifted his glass.

Livvy looked over at him, eyes wide and full of unease. She cleared her throat, telling him to stop with that look in her eyes, and he didn't even see it. He couldn't read her at all, not like I could.

At first, it was like a movie. When you knew something bad was about to happen. However, the anticipation of knowing what was coming was stronger than the ability to stop it.

I couldn't stop it.

I couldn't stop this.

His hand tucked a strand of hair behind her ear, and his fingers brushed down her cheek. "Baby, I just want your family to know how happy I am to be here with you."

A quick grimace crossed her face. It was subtle, but I noticed.

I noticed everything.

Especially when it came to her.

The whole room ate up his every last word in some sort of bullshit cosmic energy.

Fuck him.

When my eyes landed on Livvy's, it was all over as hers stayed fixated on mine. This trance was unlike anything I'd ever felt with her before. We'd been doing this dance with our eyes for as long as I could remember.

This one was definitely different.

This one hurt badly.

This one felt like it destroyed.

I was almost positive she sent me a sad smile, but I may have imagined that as our stares stayed locked, nothing, or no one, for that matter, could ever break that between us.

I had that.

It belonged to *me*.

I spent the rest of the night avoiding her. Avoiding everyone. I was like a ticking time bomb. The more I saw all of her family fawn over Beau, the more I felt like I would blow the fuck up. Shortly after dinner, I excused myself and left, briefly kissing Livvy's cheek before I did.

I barely slept that night, tossing and turning. Every time I shut my eyes, I envisioned her with him. I tried to block those images out of my mind and think about all the memories we shared.

Except it didn't help.

Before I knew it, the sun was up, and I was out of bed, showering and getting dressed. I grabbed some coffee at the shop around the corner from my apartment, and as much as I tried to ignore the thoughts of her and him, it was no use. They took up permanent residence in my head, and it didn't help that when I found myself driving to our waterhole, I stopped dead in my tracks as soon as I came up behind her.

Livvy was facing the water.

She didn't turn, softly expressing, "You weren't supposed to be there last night."

"Here I thought you'd be happy to see me."

"Ethan—"

"I hate him. He's a pretentious dick."

"That's not fair."

"None of this is fair. Your father seemed to love him, though. I wonder why that is? Maybe it's his last name?"

She immediately turned to face me. "I didn't know Beau was the son of Hunter Oil when we met."

Getting right down to it, I questioned, "How long have you been together?"

She shrugged. "A few months."

"And you didn't tell me?"

"We're just dating, Ethan. There's nothing to tell."

"You're just dating, but you bring him home to meet your parents?"

"His parents live in Summerville."

"So he spends Thanksgiving with you instead of them? Sounds pretty damn serious to me."

"They were out of town, but he's spending the week with them. It's the only reason he came to my parents with me. I would have told you I was bringing him, but you said you would be in Kansas with your uncle."

"I guess we both had surprises for each other, then."

"Ethan, don't act so innocent. I know you're dating girls, and you don't see me giving you shit about it."

"Because I told you I was! That's what best friends usually do."

"You're right. I should have told you, but like I said, we're just dating, and I didn't want to say anything to you until I knew if it'd become something more serious."

Unable to hold back, I snapped, "Are you fucking him?"

Her breathing hitched, and it was the only answer I needed.

"You're fucking other girls," she stated as if that mattered to me.

"Exactly! I fuck, Livvy. I don't fall in love."

"I don't love him."

"Yet," I bit. "You don't love him yet, but pretty boy Beau is sure as shit in love with you."

"You don't know that." She shook her head. "I don't even know that."

"You're so beautiful that it literally hurts my eyes to look at you. Trust me, I know." I paused, letting my words sink in. "Is he why you cut your hair, or did you do that because you know how much I love it?"

"I cut it because I was tired of looking in the mirror at the girl who's your best friend. I'm just trying to find my own identity."

"Are you happy? Are you happy with him?" I had to know.

She didn't reply for what felt like forever until she finally did but just nodding.

"Is he good to you?"

She nodded again, frowning. "Beau isn't the first guy I've dated since I moved to California."

"He's just the first guy you didn't tell me about, but he is the first guy you've fucked since me. Now that much I do know."

"Are you trying to hurt me?"

I didn't hesitate to confirm, "No."

LIVVY

"He's everything your father wants for you."

He stepped toward me, and I immediately stepped back. Which made him stop and cock his head to the side. "Scared of me?"

"Of course not."

"Then why won't you let me touch you? Because the second I put my hands on you, you'll know who you really belong to?"

"That's enough!"

"It doesn't make it any less true."

My chest heaved with each word that fell from his lips.

"Let me touch you, Livvy. Let me prove to you that everything I say is true."

He came at me, but this time, I expected it, so when my back hit the tree where my swing was, he instantly caged me in with his arms. His face was now mere inches away from mine. I felt him everywhere and all at once.

His scent.

His body.

His eyes.

His mouth.

Although the only thing that touched me was his arms.

"Tell me to leave, Livvy. Tell me to go. Tell me to stop."

"Ethan," I warned in a voice I didn't recognize.

He placed his forehead on mine, bringing his arms closer to frame my face. "Tell me," he groaned, making my stomach flutter and my body warm.

His mouth was so close to mine that I could feel his breath. As if testing me, he licked his lips, slowly, only provoking me.

He proved to me that he was right.

I shut my eyes. I had to. The realization was too hard to admit, and I knew he could see it in my eyes.

He knew me.

"Ethan," I panted, my breathing mimicking his. "Please..."

He rasped like he hung on by a thread, "Please what, Livvy?"

I turned my face.

"That's what I thought." He instantly backed away from me, and I felt the loss of his warmth, his love.

I stepped toward him, but now it was his turn to back away.

"Ethan..."

He smiled sadly. "As long as you're happy, that's all that truly matters to me."

I forced back the tears that wanted to escape. I would not cry. I was supposed to be happy. Beau makes me happy.

Then why do I feel like I'm dying?

I spent the past two years trying to forget about our summer together, and I couldn't until I met Beau. Except I didn't tell Ethan that. I know why I didn't...

Yes, I do.

A huge part of me was terrified that if I told Ethan I was falling for someone else, I'd be giving him the okay that he could as well. I knew that was a selfish reason, but it was there, nonetheless.

Reading my mind, he started walking back toward his truck. Never taking his intense stare off mine.

Even when he asked, "Still my girl?"

I didn't waver in replying...

"Always."

Chapter Sixteen
LIVVY

TWENTY-TWO YEARS OLD

Beau argued, "It's him, isn't it?"

"No, it's not because of Ethan."

"Bullshit. Everything is because of Ethan."

"Beau, that's not true."

"Livvy, we've been together for over two years, and he still calls you at all hours of the night. Not to mention, the number of times you two text during the day is fucking ridiculous."

"He's my best friend."

"So you've said, over and over again. I'm sick of not coming first."

"Beau, you do come first. When do I not put you first?"

"Every single time you put him first instead. I can't believe you missed dinner with my parents. You knew they were only in town for the weekend."

"I know... I'm sorry, but Ethan needed me to help him with something. I didn't do it on purpose, and I didn't know that dinner with your parents was that important."

"They wanted to see you, Liv. Do you have any idea how embarrassing it was to just sit there at dinner and for you not to show up?"

"I lost track of time. I'm sorry."

We stood in my apartment, fighting in the kitchen.

"I'm tired of all your apologies. Especially because most of them center around your so-called best friend."

"What's that supposed to mean?"

"You know exactly what it means. You never take that fucking necklace he gave you off. You know, this is just icing on the cake. You're pissed at me for calling you out on your excuses again."

"They aren't excuses. Ethan's about to launch his new app, and he needed—"

"I don't give a fuck what he needed! You're my girlfriend, not his! Or do I need to remind you who you belong to?"

I jerked back, remembering Ethan saying those same words to me that morning after Thanksgiving at our waterhole.

"I... I..."

"You need to decide who comes first, Liv. If it's not going to be me, then I refuse to play second fiddle to that asshole."

I gasped. "He's not an asshole!"

"That's what you decide to focus on? You're truly unbelievable. Ethan is an asshole. You think I don't notice his snarky remarks to me or the way he looks at you blatantly in front of me? You say nothing happened between you two, but your close friendship screams otherwise."

I never told Beau about what I now called "The Summer." He didn't need to know. Nobody did. Besides, it was none of his business. The last thing I needed was for him to lose his shit more than he was lately in reference to Ethan.

"We're just best friends," I stated for what felt like the millionth time.

"You think I'm that stupid? You think I can't tell he's been inside you?"

"Beau—"

"I'd even go as far as to say that you two probably lost your virginity to each other, right? He was probably your first kiss too?"

"You need to calm down."

"You're not answering me, and you think that's going to make me calm down?"

"What kind of question is that? It sounds more like a threat than anything else."

"It's a simple question, don't you think?"

"I'm going to ask this one last time and please, please, be honest with me. Do you love me, Liv?"

I stepped in front of him, grabbing his face. "You know I do."

"Actually, I don't." With that, he jerked his head away from my grasp. "I need a break."

"What?" I snapped, narrowing my eyes at him.

"This can't come as a surprise to you."

"What are you saying?"

"I'm saying I need some space. Don't call me. Don't come to my place. Just leave me alone until you figure out where I come in your life."

"You don't mean that."

"I do. I've never meant anything more in my life."

Before I could reply, he turned and left, slamming the door behind him.

Was he right? Did I put Ethan before him?

I spent the rest of the night going stir-crazy, trying to figure out if what he accused me of was true. I did love him. I wouldn't be with him this long if I didn't. I hated that he didn't trust me. For the next few days, I moved in autopilot until I couldn't resist.

I needed my best friend, so I ended up at his front door. I didn't tell him I was coming, booking a last-minute flight late at night. It was past three in the morning when I stood there. Instead of knocking, I decided to surprise him.

Using the key he gave me a long time ago, I quietly made my way inside, tiptoeing through his place. Once I was at his bedroom door, I was just going to sneak into his bed with him. Except my timing was shit. As soon as I stepped inside, the full moon cascaded along his body, and I could see him and the naked woman in bed with him.

"Fuck," I breathed out. Backing away, I felt my heart in my throat.

I'd never seen him with anyone prior to this. I knew he dated, but he never brought them around. I guess I thought...

I don't know what I thought.

Question after question tore through my mind.

Is that his girlfriend? Does he love her? How long have they been sleeping together? Does he always let women spend the night?

The last question didn't end before the next one began, and God chose that second to make a mockery out of me. I wasn't paying attention to where I was stepping, quickly trying to get out of his room. In my rush, I tripped over what felt like his shoes.

In a loud, hard thud, I fell on my ass and immediately woke them up. Ethan jumped out of bed, making me realize he was butt-ass naked too. My wide gaze flew from his shocked expression to seeing me there to his big dick that wasn't even hard, dangling between his legs.

"Fuck," I repeated, covering my eyes. "I'm so sorry."

"Livvy," he uttered in a husky yet sleepy tone.

"I... I..."

"Ethan," the chick announced, sitting up. "What's going on?"

"Uh... I'm so sorry. I didn't know he was with someone. I... I... shit..." I jumped up, and my best friend still hadn't covered himself.

Stop staring at his dick, Livvy.

"I'm going to go." I spun, hauling ass out of there.

"Livvy!" Ethan called out after me, but it was no use.

I was already opening the front door when he gripped my arm, turning me to face him. Thank God, he at least threw on his gym shorts. However, him being shirtless wasn't helping my disposition either. I hadn't seen him since spring break when he spent the week at my apartment with me, and that was almost six months ago.

How can he look better than the last time I saw him?

His black hair was messy from sleep, framing pieces of his face. His usual bright blue was a soft colored teal while his strong jawline and pouty lips were prominent from sleep too. His body appeared better than I remembered and that V above his happy trail still had the power to knock me senseless.

I shook my head, trying to turn around again. "I shouldn't be here."

He held me in place. "What are you doing here?"

I blurted, "Beau and I broke up and I just needed you."

"Oh, Livvy." He pulled me into a tight hug. "Are you okay?"

"Yeah." I nodded, hugging him back for a second.

He smelled so fucking good.

"I should go, and you should go... you know, back to your date or whatever."

He chuckled. "She's just a girl. You're always more important."

"I don't think she's going to appreciate that."

"She doesn't matter. She knows where we stand."

"Ummm... okay."

Why does that make me feel better?

"Come on." Ethan grabbed my hand, leading me to his back porch.

He turned on the warm hanging lights before he pulled out a chair for me to sit in. I sat down but out of the corner of my eyes I watched the woman who was in bed with him leave out his front door.

"She's probably going to hate me now."

"Don't worry about her," he stressed in one breath. "She's no one."

I eyed him skeptically. "If you weren't my best friend, I'd call you an asshole."

"Well." He grinned, sitting in the seat in front of me across the table. "Good thing I am, then."

"So... women are just cool with this setup you have going? The wham bam, thank you, ma'am?"

He smiled. "I guess so."

"Huh... that's nice for you," I sarcastically stated. "Is she the only one who sleeps over, or do you have slumber parties with all of them?"

"Livvy, you're not here to talk about my sex life. Now what's going on?"

I scratched my head, hating that he ignored my question. "I missed dinner with Beau's parents because I was helping you with your app launch, and it spiraled into something else entirely."

He arched an eyebrow. "If you had told me you had plans with his family, I would have understood."

"Would you?"

He cocked his head to the side.

"Beau says that I put you first before him. More like I put you first before anyone."

"I see."

It was my turn to cock my head. "Do you?"

He shrugged. "I'm not sure what you want me to say."

"The truth."

"Livvy, we're best friends. At the end of the day, I was here before him, and I'll be here after him."

"Then you knew there'd be an after?"

"Are you asking me if I wanted you two to break up?"

"Did you?"

In one sentence, he reminded me, "I just want you to be happy."

And for the first time, I hated hearing him say that too.

ETHAN

This was not how I expected to be woken up, but I'd be lying if I said I wasn't ecstatic to see her. I'd also be lying if I said I wasn't glad they broke up. Despite Beau being from the elite status that her father always wanted for her, in my eyes, he wasn't good enough for her.

To be completely honest, I couldn't for the life of me see what she saw in him. To me, he was a pompous prick born with a silver spoon in his mouth. I still couldn't stand him, but I tolerated him for her. For some reason I couldn't begin to understand, she loved him. Or at least that was what she said, and it could have been entirely true.

However, I didn't think she was in love with him.

Not for one fucking second.

Livvy was always a hopeless romantic. She loved love, and at that point in our lives, she looked for it in all the wrong places. Case in point: Beau Hunter.

The bane of my existence. She might have known that—she might have known a lot of things, but in order to stay best friends and not mess up our friendship again, we stayed in our own lanes. Meaning, I was there for her whenever she needed me and vice versa. If she wanted to continue being in that relationship, my job was to support her.

Livvy was a big girl. She could make her own decisions despite how much I hated him for her.

"I can see your mind spinning, Ethan."

"Did I say a word?"

"No, but your expression yells for you. I know you want to say 'I told you so.'"

"Or maybe you just want to hear me say it."

"I know you don't like Beau."

"What's there to like?"

She scoffed out a chuckle. "You're shameless."

"And you wouldn't have it any other way."

"Do you think he's right? Do I put you before him?"

"Livvy, I just kicked a woman out of my bed because you unexpectedly showed up in my bedroom at three in the morning. I think it's safe to say you're asking the wrong person."

"I thought you said she knew where you stood?"

"She does, but it doesn't make it any less true."

"Are you saying you agree with him?"

"I'm not saying I don't."

She sighed deeply.

"Is that not what you want to hear?"

"I don't know what I want to hear."

"Then maybe we just need to dance."

"Ethan..."

I stood, grabbing her phone to play one of her favorite songs. Putting her cell back on the table, I dragged her up from her seat and proceeded to wrap her in my arms. Effortlessly, we began slow dancing. Through the course of our friendship, if there was one thing that made Livvy smile, it was slow dancing with me.

She melted into my embrace, laying her head on my chest as I tucked her under my chin.

"This isn't why I came here," she lied.

"This is exactly why you came here," I spoke the truth.

We stayed like that, dancing under the full moon and stars.

Both of us lost in our own thoughts.

In our own demons.

"How do you always make me feel better?"

I smiled, kissing the top of her head and letting my lips linger until she peered up at me through her long, dark lashes.

For the first time, she asked, "Am I still your girl?"

And I didn't falter in reassuring her. "Always."

Meaning it from the bottom of my heart.

Chapter Seventeen

ETHAN

TWENTY-FOUR YEARS OLD

"You did it! I'm so freaking proud of you, Ethan! Your app is number one!" Livvy shouted over the crowds of people at our launch party.

My partners and investors decided they wanted to celebrate with hundreds of their closest friends. Some of them I'd met, most I hadn't. I wasn't much for bars or clubs, let alone parties on my behalf. For the past two years, I lived and breathed my social media app, where I was the president, owning 51 percent of the company. My goal was to eventually buy everyone out and be the sole owner. Until then, I was grateful for their help in getting it going.

I couldn't believe that it only took twenty-four hours for the app to be number one on all platforms. I definitely wasn't expecting that. I was just trying to keep my head above water.

From the reporters.

To the bloggers.

To the endless interviews, news stations, and all of the magazines that wanted a piece of me.

I hated being the center of attention, and now I was in the spotlight whether I wanted to be.

Once we were alone, standing outside on the balcony of the hotel, Livvy announced, "Ethan, did you see all the paparazzi downstairs who are chomping at the bit to snap a photo of you?"

"Yeah." That was all I could say.

"How are you not ecstatic right now? You're going to become the next big thing! Did you see the article that Forbes wrote about you? They're saying you'll be the next billionaire and Fortune 500 company!"

"Yeah," I repeated in the same tone.

"That's all you can say?"

"Livvy, I hate all this publicity, and you know that."

"I know, but this is such a huge deal. I can't believe my best friend is on his way to becoming one of the richest men in the world, and you're only twenty-four years old!"

I smiled. "I do appreciate your enthusiasm, but I have no interest in being friends with the press."

"Have you taken a good look at yourself in the mirror lately? Women all around the world are already obsessed with you, and this is only the beginning of your career. I can't imagine what it will be like in a year."

"What does that have to do with anything?"

"Umm... sex sells, and you're totally going to be the next Hollywood It Guy."

"Not if I have anything to say about it."

She shrugged. "I think you'll have to get used to the attention and possibly hire a bodyguard. At least twenty reporters are waiting for you outside the hotel. What do you think it's going to be like from this point forward? It's only going to get worse."

"I'm not sure," I admitted. "I didn't think about any of this. I just wanted to develop my app."

"Ethan." She beamed. "You were our valedictorian. You graduated in the top 5 percent of your class at university. I always knew you'd accomplish everything you set out to do, and I couldn't be prouder of you right now. The press is not going to leave you alone, especially after *Time* magazine did that article on you. Did you read that one at least?"

"No."

"Ethan! How can you be this oblivious to what everyone writes about you? How can you be any more oblivious about how handsome you are and the effect you have on women? Just that, by itself, will skyrocket you into fame. Not to mention, you're a fucking genius."

I really did love her support. "I should hire you to do my PR."

She giggled, and it was still one of my favorite sounds.

"You know what you should do?"

"No, but you're sure as shit going to tell me."

She rolled her eyes. "Rude, but I'll forgive you. You should release a statement on your app that says you want people to respect your privacy during this transition in your life. That may help."

"Look at you, just full of good ideas."

"I'm a very smart girl. Plus, I love pop culture, so I've been preparing for this my entire life."

"Are you going to hang posters of me on your walls too?"

She smirked, remembering all the pictures she'd rip out of her magazines that she'd tape to her walls. There wasn't an actor or singer who hadn't been displayed in her bedroom from the ages of ten to fourteen.

"If you're lucky," she playfully teased, leaning onto the railing with me. She nudged my shoulder. "I am really proud of you, though."

"I know." I nudged her shoulder back.

"What are you going to do with your first million?"

"Buy out my investors."

She chuckled. "You don't want to share?"

"Not if I can help it."

"I love that you're accomplishing all your goals. With my father running for governor this year, he wants me to join his team after I get my law degree."

I arched an eyebrow, tapering my stare at her. "You want to work for your old man?"

"Hardly, but you know him… he always gets what he wants."

"Livvy, you're a grown-ass woman who can make your own decisions now."

"If that were true, I wouldn't be in law school."

"Oh yeah? What would you be doing?"

"It's stupid."

"Try me."

"No." She shook her head. "You'll think it's dumb."

"So you're keeping secrets from me now?"

She blushed.

"The suspense is killing me, Livvy."

"Ethan, this is your night. Why are we even talking about me?"

"I'm still waiting."

"Fine." She sighed deeply, hesitating for a moment. "I've always been a hopeless romantic. I just thought I'd get married young, and I don't know, maybe have some kids already."

My eyebrows lowered. "You've never told me that."

"I know, it's because it's silly."

"Who are you marrying?"

"What?"

"You heard me."

She weighed her words, aware I wouldn't like who she revealed.

"I guess... for a while, I thought it'd be Beau."

They'd been on and off for the past two years.

Reeling in my emotions, I bit, "Are you guys back together again?" in a harsh voice.

"I know you're not his biggest fan."

"That's putting it mildly."

"Ethan, we're just talking."

"You're always just talking."

The son of a bitch would not let her go. He was adamant about keeping her in his life, and as much as I hated to admit it, Livvy did love him, and for the most part, he was good to her. If he weren't, I would have already broken his fucking legs.

"Are you not seeing anyone special?" she questioned out of nowhere, changing the subject.

"Am I ever seeing anyone special?"

"Good point." She smiled.

I tugged on her red hair. "You're the only special girl I need."

"Don't you ever get lonely?"

"Lonely isn't a word I'd use to describe myself."

"How about man whore?"

I chuckled. "That's two words."

"Don't you ever get tired of sleeping with random women all the time?"

"Livvy, I was a virgin until I was almost nineteen. I'm just making up for lost time," I teased.

She scoffed. "You're such a guy."

"If I were that guy, I'd say something like I have plenty of women who keep my bed warm on rotation."

Her mouth dropped open, slapping my chest. "Ethan Carter!"

I laughed, grabbing her shoulder and giving it a gentle squeeze. "I'm kidding."

"No, you're not, and that's what makes it worse. How many women have you been with?"

I grinned, squeezing her shoulder again. "A gentleman never tells."

"Is that your way of saying a hundred?"

"Oh, come on. You can't possibly think I've fucked a hundred women in six years?"

"Yeah, I can." She adamantly nodded. "That's only like one woman a month."

I jerked back, considering it before nodding in agreement. "Well, shit. You learn something new every day."

"So how many is it?"

"I mean, more than one a month."

Her face scrunched.

"You asked."

"Yeah, but the fact that you just realized how many women you've actually indeed fucked is alarming."

"Don't ask questions you don't want the answers to."

"You know what?"

"What, Livvy?"

All in one breath, she spoke with conviction, "You're right."

Chapter Eighteen
LIVVY

TWENTY-SIX YEARS OLD

I started my day by drinking a full glass of warm lemon water while I leaned over the island in my apartment, going through my emails as I waited for Ethan's plane to land. I was still living in California, and Ethan owned one of his headquarters for his app in LA. Despite having all the money in the world, he stayed at my place anytime he was in town.

I grabbed my yoga mat to exercise on my living room floor. I slipped on my Bluetooth headphones, shaking out my head for the anxiety I was suddenly feeling. Getting into position on my mat, I faced the foam and went into downward dog position with my butt in the air.

Lifting my leg in the air next, I pressed my shoulder blades into the mat, deeply breathing out at the same time, and already, the elephant on my chest lightened up. Swiftly, I changed into a standing straddle, forward bend. Grabbing onto the back of my ankles, I pulled my chest as close as it would go under my legs. I'd been doing yoga since I began college and been addicted ever since.

Never once did I open my eyes, knowing the mat by my memory alone. Slowly, I slid to the ground and lay on my back. Raising my hips to the air, I stretched my lower back, once again releasing another solid breath. Pumping my hips up and down a few times, I inhaled in and out. Making sure to feel the strain the movement triggered in my muscles.

Gripping the inner sides of my feet, I got into the ananda balasana pose, which basically looked like an upside-down frog. Letting my breathing go long and deep, I was about to change positions.

Except when I opened my eyes for the first time, I loudly gasped, causing my butt to wiggle in this extremely sexual position.

"How long have you been standing there?"

Ethan smiled, bright and bold. "Long enough to feel like I should be throwing money at you, but instead, I'm just enjoying the free show."

I let go of my feet and shot up. "You're horrible. Your plane must have landed early."

"I love the welcome I come home to. Maybe next time, you should do yoga in a bikini instead."

"You wish," I baited.

"That little number you're wearing doesn't leave much to the imagination."

I was in a sports bra and spandex booty shorts.

"I thought I was alone."

"Here I thought this warm welcome was for me, but don't stop on my behalf. I can help you stretch those tight muscles. You know, get you nice and wet if you need me to."

"Ethan!"

"What?" He innocently shrugged. "Sweating is good for you."

I smirked at him.

"Do you know that you make sex noises when you're doing what you call yoga, right?"

"I do not."

"I'm very familiar with your sex noises, Livvy. You could probably call me a pro, considering I taught you everything you love."

My eyes widened. "Have you been drinking? What's with the trip down memory lane?"

"It doesn't have to be a memory."

I cocked my head to the side. "What's gotten into you?"

He grinned, eyeing me up and down. "If you keep making noises like that, I'll happily show you."

I couldn't help it. I burst out laughing.

"There's my girl. I missed you."

"I guess I kind of missed you," I taunted.

He laughed, throwing his head back. His laughter was always so contagious. Making my way back into the kitchen, I was about to open the fridge when he grabbed my waist from behind and tugged me into his rock-hard chest.

"Ethan, I'm all sweaty."

He murmured into my neck, "I like you all sweaty," before he kissed it and let me go. "I just wanted a hug."

I giggled. "I'm going to go shower."

"Do you need any help in there too?"

"Oh, look at you," I jokingly mocked. "You're just trying to be so helpful this morning."

"What can I say? I'm a gentleman."

"Oh yeah? Mr. Forbes Most Eligible Bachelor. I think they use the term 'play billionaire' in reference to you."

"I've been called worse, but they have to sell magazines, don't they?"

"And as we all know." I gestured to him. "Your face always sells. I can't go into the grocery store without seeing a tabloid with you and some model of the week on it."

He shamelessly shrugged. "They're not always models. Besides, most of that is bullshit lies."

"Oh, so you weren't just in Bali with Varissa Gilati? Isn't she the top-grossing model this year?"

He ignored my question. "It was a work trip."

"On a private yacht with a supermodel?"

"It's not very private if you know about it."

"Is it serious?"

"Livvy, is it ever serious with anyone?"

"One day, you're going to be serious about someone."

"I don't have time for any of that."

"I guess that's what happens when your app goes public, Mr. Billionaire. I still can't believe *The* Ethan Carter is in my apartment."

"Don't let the tabloid bullshit get to you. I'm still the same man I always was."

"I know, I'm just teasing you. What kind of best friend would I be if I didn't give you shit for how the world loves you."

"I don't need the world to love."

"But they do even though your personality doesn't exactly speak highly for itself. Especially in the media's eyes."

"Well, that's not my fucking problem. I have no interest in performing for the public like I need my dick stroked. I'm just a businessman, Livvy. I make money, and that's all anyone needs to know."

Hearing him talk to me with so much confident authority made me realize that my best friend had new sides of him I hadn't seen yet. For a moment, that made me sad.

He must have noticed it because he ordered, "Enough about me. What's new with you?"

I hadn't talked to him in a few weeks. He was overseas with supermodels, apparently.

Giving in to his demands, I replied, "I'm still looking for a job."

For some reason, it made me think about how easily it was for everyone else to march in line with what he ordered.

"You want to be my lawyer?"

"How often do you need one?"

"Enough to have three on the payroll."

"Hmm..." I lifted my finger to my lip. "You're not wealthy unless someone tries to sue you every day."

"Yeah, something like that."

I hated feeling like I didn't know this part of him. Instead of lingering on those emotions, I shoved them away and showered. Never expecting or predicting what would come later that night.

Not for one damn second.

ETHAN

I went to the LA office most of the day and then had dinner with some business prospects. I thought about Livvy the entire time. There was something in her eyes from that morning that I couldn't forget. It was almost as if she didn't recognize me anymore, which made no sense. She was the only person in the world who knew me.

When I returned to her apartment, I needed to tell her what I came to say. Now after all these years, maybe it was the time to explore what we started that summer before college. Last I heard, she wasn't with Beau anymore.

I walked inside her place, using the key she gave me freshman year. The lights were off, and I turned on the one in the hallway.

"Livvy," I hollered to no avail. Next, I knocked on her bedroom door. "Livvy." Since there was no answer, I opened it.

And immediately came face-to-face with a topless Livvy.

She loudly gasped, spinning around to face me with her arms over her chest.

I instantly smiled, gripping the door handle. Cocking my head to the side, I took in her gorgeous body that looked better than I remembered.

My girl.

"Ethan! Oh my God! Turn around!"

I grinned. "It's nothing I haven't seen before."

She shook off my remark. "Were you raised in a barn? Shut the door."

"You don't have to ask me twice." I shut the door, leaning my back against it with my arms crossed over my chest.

"I meant get out," she scolded.

"But I thought we could have a slumber party."

"Can you at least shut your eyes so I can continue getting dressed?"

I lay on her bed, looking up at the ceiling for a few seconds before tossing my arm over my eyes to allow her to change. I didn't know how long I lay there until I felt the bed dip beside me.

She wore white cotton shorts with a tight white tank top. Her red hair had gotten long again, falling all the way down to her waist. This was the first time I'd seen it grown out this long since before she left for college.

Grabbing the ends, I coaxed, "Your hair is long."

I couldn't help but recall why she cut it in the first place.

"I cut it because I was tired of looking in the mirror at the girl who's your best friend. I'm just trying to find my own identity."

Her bright green eyes still had the power to bring me to my knees with a simple look. She wasn't wearing any makeup, but she never needed it. She was always naturally breathtaking. The women I hooked up with didn't even come close to her beauty.

Something in her gaze told me she wanted to say so much. Our summer still lurked right around the corner like a shadow I could never get away from. However, I never really tried to either. I chose to have it stay there in case we ever got a second chance at being together.

She caressed my cheek with the knuckles of her delicate fingers like she knew what I felt, what I thought, what I wanted. I leaned into her hand, and it fell onto the back of the headboard. I used it as a pillow as her other hand played with my hair, pulling the longer pieces away from my face.

My face turned into the palm of her hand, and I softly kissed it before I slowly placed tender kisses up her arm, brushing my lips back and forth to enjoy the feel of her skin against my mouth.

She was so soft.

So warm.

It had been so fucking long.

Eight years felt like a lifetime ago.

Except my lock and key necklace was always on her neck.

She lightly gasped, and once I made it to her shoulder, I slid her hair to the other side of her neck, never stopping my caresses on her skin. I could feel my effect on her, and she hadn't stopped me.

"Ethan," she lightly stirred, her body tensing.

My heart sped up. "What?" I was getting closer to her neck.

"You need to stop."

"I'm just kissing my best friend."

Her chest lifted with every movement of my lips getting closer to her mouth. I grabbed the side of her face, beckoning her mouth to mine, and she let me. Her eyes were tightly closed, and she smelled like the honey that haunted my dreams every night.

"You're so fucking beautiful," I groaned, desperately craving to feel her again.

Her mouth parted as I brought her over to me. The smell and feel of her were making me dizzy, and all I wanted was to kiss her. It was such an innocent gesture, such a simple desire. I wanted to capture this moment and hold on to it for as long as I could. I wanted to remember her just this way.

For me.

Mine.

"I know a part of me will always wait for you, Livvy," I murmured, getting closer to her mouth.

She shook her head, unable to find the words.

"You've ruined me for every other woman. You know that, don't you? It's always going to be you."

She immediately opened her eyes and looked right into mine. "Ethan..."

I didn't falter. "I'll always be in lov—"

The sound of the front door opening was as if a bucket of ice-cold water was abruptly poured on my head. She jumped back and away from me after the sudden interruption.

The mistakes I couldn't change were still there.

Especially our regrets.

I stood at the same time as the person I least expected walked into her bedroom.

"There's my girl," Beau announced, grabbing the swell of her back. He pulled her into a deep kiss.

This motherfucker.

It was only then he turned around to look at me. "Hey, man. I must have got the days confused. I thought you were arriving tomorrow."

Liar.

He knew exactly what he was doing.

"That makes two of us. I thought she finally got rid of you."

"Ethan," Livvy stressed in that tone I hated when it came to him.

He scoffed out a snide chuckle. "Oh, so she didn't tell you?"

"Tell me what?"

I should have seen this coming, but then again it wouldn't have mattered. Nothing ever did when it came to her and I.

In four words, he put an end to what could have been our beginning by revealing...

"We're moving in together."

Chapter Nineteen

ETHAN

TWENTY-EIGHT YEARS OLD

"*I need you, Ethan.*"

I immediately asked, "What's with all the cryptic? Are you alright?"

"I've never been better." She paused for a moment, and I could sense her hesitation.

"You think you can take time off from work for the next week?"

"Not until you tell me why?" I cautiously waited for I don't know what.

"I just need my best friend."

I abruptly sat up, about to respond, but she would have knocked me on my ass if I wasn't already sitting down. It all happened so fast, yet it still seemed as if it played out in slow motion.

She unexpectedly revealed, "I'm getting married."

"What—"

She cut me off, bluntly adding...

"And I need you to be my man of honor."

The memory of that phone call with Livvy played on repeat in my mind for the past four days since she told me. There I was on my private plane to fucking France. The ten-hour flight was painful, to say the least, and the last hour was almost crippling.

Livvy and Beau were getting married in Château d'Esclimont Castle, and their weeklong extravagant wedding celebration began this evening with their engagement/welcome party. They had some festivity planned daily, ending with their ceremony and wedding on the last day.

Not only did I have to endure my best friend getting married to the wrong man, but I had to be fucking part of everything since I was Livvy's man of honor. She emailed me the itinerary. From the bridal party to the bridal shower to the bridal luncheon and farewell. Including the bridal and bachelor nights that were a day apart.

It was a week of pure and utter torture, and I had no clue how I would survive it. The only thing I had in mind was wanting to stop it. There was no way in hell I would let her marry that pretentious prick. Not if I could help it.

I didn't know how I would stop this fiasco of a marriage. All I knew was that I had to play nice until I could figure out what to do. I already had my entire team running background checks on the son of a bitch. There had to be something there I could use as ammo.

The more I thought of them tying the knot, the sicker I felt in the pit of my stomach. I never actually thought it would get to this point, and I couldn't for the life of me begin to understand what the fuck was happening.

For the past two years, I'd been so busy building my empire that I let her slip through my fingers. I'd only seen her once, and it was for a moment. We both had busy and intense schedules that never lined up. We still talked a couple of times a week, but even those calls were short because we were between meetings and whatever else took priority in our lives.

This was a disaster. It was the only way I could explain it. I loved Livvy more than anything in this world, and I couldn't watch her spend the rest of her life with this asshole. Let alone have children with him. Her father was governor, and I could only imagine how thrilled he was that his only daughter would be marrying into the Hunter Oil dynasty.

They were one of the richest families. Generational wealth dating back to the early nineteen hundreds. It was an empire, and their joining would get her old man ahead of the game if he decided to run for the presidency. According to Livvy, his whole team pushed for it. He'd done a lot for the state of South Carolina and was very well-loved. I wouldn't be surprised if he did.

The man's ambitions knew no bounds. I guess you could say we had that in common. The way I wanted to explode was so unfamiliar to me. I was a man who prided himself on control, and now I felt as if I didn't have any. Livvy was meant to be mine, and I'd make sure of it no matter what.

I had no fucking problem reminding her of that. It was only then that I realized what I had to do. I had to remind her of what we once had. Of what we'd always have. Of what we were to each other.

Ethan and Livvy.
Livvy and Ethan.
Best friends.
Soulmates.
Then.
Now.
Forever.
Because at the end of the day...
She was mine first.

LIVVY

I stared at myself in the mirror, inhaling a deep breath. I wore a floor-length white satin dress that clung to my body like a second skin. It accentuated all of my curves with a deep V in the back. My red hair flowed loosely, reaching almost my ass. The makeup artist went heavy on the eye makeup and bright red lip.

Hundreds of people were flying in from all over the world for our weeklong celebration. Our families weren't too excited about us wanting to get married immediately, but with the power of both our families, it wasn't hard for them to accomplish it. The castle would be filled with our invitees in less than an hour. I barely knew a handful of people, yet our wedding was reaching 1500 guests.

Politicians.

CEOs.

And God knows who else.

The elite on our guest list was endless.

The Château d'Esclimont Castle must have cost a fortune to rent out for the week. Everything would take place here, and although I was excited to become Mrs. Hunter, I was also nervous about what was to come. This was the storybook wedding every little girl dreamed of, including myself.

Beau was truly making all my dreams come true, and I loved him for it.

When he asked me to marry him a few nights ago, I'd be lying if I said I expected it. We'd been on and off for the past ten years. The past two were probably the best of our entire relationship. After we got back together the last time, I think we both changed in regard to what the other was looking for.

Beau didn't ride my ass about Ethan anymore, but maybe it was because we hadn't really seen one another other more than briefly, one time, in the past two years. We still talked quite often, though, yet he no longer gave me a hard time about that. I felt as if he finally accepted that Ethan was my best friend, and he wouldn't ever come between that.

Beau knew his role in my life. He was my number one and always a top priority to me. However, Ethan was right there beside him. They were both the men in my life, and I wouldn't have it any other way, regardless.

Seconds later, Beau suddenly came up behind me and wrapped his arm around my waist.

"You look so breathtaking, sweetheart. I don't think I've ever seen you look more beautiful than you do right now. I can't wait to see you in your wedding gown if this is what you look like for our engagement/welcome party this evening."

I smiled at him through the mirror. "You don't look so bad yourself in that tuxedo, Mr. Hunter."

"This old thing," he teased, winking at me through the reflection. "Why, thank you, Mrs. Hunter."

"I'm not Mrs. Hunter yet."

"I'm just practicing. Have I told you how much I love that you'll be my wife?"

I smiled, enjoying his affection.

"Till death do us part, Elizabeth." He kissed my neck. "Have you found your wedding gown?"

"Not yet, but our mothers are scouring the country for it. Tomorrow morning, they're holding me hostage to find the perfect one."

"Are you going to the bridal shops?"

"No, they're bringing them here."

"That sounds like our mothers."

"They have become rather close in such a short amount of time."

"They're spending money. It's what my mother does best."

"Touché."

"I'm taking the men golfing for most of the morning, but I'll be back in the afternoon to fuck you before lunch."

"Beau." I snickered, shaking my head.

"What? You're lucky I don't take you right now as you're looking at us in the mirror."

"Don't you dare," I warned. "This dress costs a fortune, and you can't be ruining it."

"I can buy you another one. I can buy you whatever you want."

"I can buy myself whatever I want to."

"I know, sweetheart. It's one of the things I love the most about you. Your independence, your strength, your determination to succeed when you could just be a trust fund baby to your daddy."

"Bite your tongue."

"How about you bite it for me?"

"And mess up my lipstick? We can't have that now."

He smirked, kissing his way down my neck before bringing up my hair. "I think you should have the stylist put your hair up to show off your sexy as sin, naked back."

A glam squad was paid around the clock to be there for me and our mothers, which probably cost a small fortune, along with a videographer and photographer. For the next week, we'd have a whole team of people following us to ensure we had everything we needed.

"You think?" I asked, still staring at him through the mirror. "I thought you loved my hair down?"

"I do, but for this occasion and this dress." He nodded to it. "Your hair should be up to show off these diamond earrings." With that, he slid what appeared to be new jewelry on my ears.

I lightly gasped, looking at the dangling diamonds that must have been three or four carats on their own.

"Matches your ring," he added, kissing my hand.

There, shining prominently on my ring finger, was my five-carat oval diamond engagement ring,

"Oh my God, Beau. This is too much."

"Nothing is too much for my wife-to-be, Mrs. Hunter."

Before I could argue, he placed a diamond pendant necklace around my neck and a diamond-encrusted tennis bracelet on my wrist.

"Beau…"

"They belonged to my mother," he murmured in my ear. "She wore them for her wedding day and passed them down to me to give to my future bride when I turned twenty-one. They're yours now, darling."

"You can't be serious. This is millions of dollars in jewelry."

"Get used to it, Mrs. Hunter. They're many more years of diamonds to come."

My eyes widened. "How did I get so lucky?"

He spun me to face him. "I'm the lucky one."

He kissed me deeply, passionately, not caring about my red lipstick. All of a sudden, this physical ache surrounded me, consuming me for a moment. Our gravitational pull toward each other was alive and present, taking control of me.

I felt him from across the bridal suite in this castle built for a king and queen. There in the arms of my fiancé, I locked stares with the boy I'd known since I was six years old. Twenty-two years later, my boy had become a man, wearing his own black tuxedo suit.

He'd forever own a huge piece of my heart.

A big part of my soul.

With one look, with no words, he was able to remind me of how much I loved him for always being there for me, and this was no exception.

I swallowed hard, taking in for the first time in what felt like an eternity...

My best friend.

My man of honor.

My first love.

Ethan Carter.

Chapter Twenty
LIVVY

Beau excused himself to answer a call. Not noticing Ethan stood under the doorframe of my bridal suite as he left out the other door. I grabbed my mouth, turning to see if my lips were a mess, and to my surprise, they weren't one bit. The makeup artist did say they were kiss-proof, and we proved that theory.

Once I spun around to look at Ethan, he had already closed the distance between us. Quickly catching me off guard, I stumbled back and lost my footing. One second, I stood in the arms of my fiancé, and the next, I stood in the embrace of my best friend.

Placing my hand on his firm chest, I rasped, "These stiletto heels will take some getting used to."

"Don't worry. I'm here to catch you if you fall."

I nervously chuckled, clearing my throat before gaining my composure to stand on my own. After I stepped away, he caressed the side of my face.

"You look stunning, Livvy. White has always been my favorite color on you for a reason."

"Thank you." I blushed, bowing my head for a moment before grabbing the lapels of his jacket. "I think the last time I saw you in a tux was prom night."

With only one sentence out of my mouth, I threw us back to another place and time where I was once only his.

Shaking off the memories, I added, "How was your flight?"

He realized my sudden discomfort, and I knew he also remembered that night.

He called me out on it and replied, "You were wearing white on prom night too."

"Yeah." I patted down the front of my satin dress, making sure the fabric didn't wrinkle. "But it wasn't a Vera Wang, twenty-thousand-dollar dress."

"When did you start caring about designers?"

"I don't. Beau picked this dress out for me, and I just happened to see the cost while I was trying it on for him in the dressing room."

"I see," he stated in a stern tone. "He has great taste. You look exquisite. Timeless. I'm actually finding it hard to breathe in your presence."

"You always know the right things to say."

"I'm just being honest."

"I'm not the only one wearing designer." I smiled. "I recognize an Armani tuxedo when I see it. I've seen it on my father enough through the years. You look great, Ethan. Truly. You're all grown up now. I feel like I'm seeing you for the first time in years, and I hardly recognize you despite seeing your face everywhere."

"Even your dreams?"

I smirked. "Still charming as I ever, I see."

"What can I say?" He beamed. "You bring out the best in me."

"Ditto."

He nodded to the jewelry I was wearing. "Will there be an armed guard following you around for the night?"

"You'd think so, right? Actually, at this point, probably. However, it was Beau's mother's, and now it's mine, I guess."

He eyed me up and down with almost a hurt expression, I knew what he was looking for that was missing from my neck.

"You'd think he was trying to buy your affection or something?"

"He doesn't have to do that, Ethan. I'd love him without any diamonds."

He narrowed his intense stare at me. "Says the woman who just used past tense to say how much she loves her fiancé."

I glared at him, and he lifted his hands in the air in a surrendering gesture.

"What kind of best friend would I be if I didn't joke at your fiancé's expense?"

"You're not joking. I know you don't like him."

"What's not to like? I'm here for you, aren't I? Although." He moved his finger around the suite. "I wasn't expecting a fairy-tale wedding in a castle of all places. It just doesn't seem like the girl I know."

"A lot can change in two years."

"Are you happy?" he asked out of nowhere. "I just want you to be happy, Livvy."

"Are you happy, Ethan?" I countered, throwing his own question back at him.

"Is there a reason you're avoiding my question?"

"No. Of course, I'm happy. I'm getting married to the man I'm in love with."

He eyed me up and down again.

"Stop looking at me like that."

He played innocent. "Like what?"

"Like I'm a trophy you hang on a wall."

A small smile spread across his lips. "If the heel fits, Mrs. Hunter."

I winced. It was quick, but he saw it.

"It's not like that between Beau and me. You've read us all wrong. You know my father will probably run for president, and this is just his way of showing off."

"Still living your life for your old man, Livvy?"

"That's not what I meant."

"Not in so many words, but that's what you just said."

"What do you expect from me, Ethan? What do you want from me?"

"You know what I want," he openly shared. "You've known since we were kids, and I surprised you with our waterhole one morning. It hasn't changed. It never changes between us. You know that as much as I do. You may be marrying another man, but we both know who you belong to. Remember, Livvy… you once promised me that you'd never forget that you were mine first."

I gasped, stepping back. "That's uncalled for."

At that moment, I hated that he knew so much about me.

I hated that our childhoods were entwined together like the weaving of a tightrope.

I hated that I couldn't think of one experience that didn't involve him in it.

But most of all, I hated that he did indeed claim all my firsts.

"It doesn't make it any less true."

"Stop it," I ordered, shaking my head in disappointment.

"I know you inside and out, so stop pretending I don't."

I was about to respond, but he breathed out, "Do you love him more than me?"

"That's not fair," I argued, trying to control the emotions threatening to take over.

"You're right. If life were fair, then you'd be marrying—"

"Ethan," Beau interrupted, abruptly walking into the room. As soon as he stood beside me, he laid his hand on the swell of my back. "Glad to see you could make it." He glanced at me for a second. "Doesn't my girl Livvy look gorgeous?"

My eyebrows pinched together. He'd never called me Livvy before. Nobody called me that but Ethan. We locked eyes, and I could see that Ethan had the same thought as I did.

"Yes," Ethan agreed. "My girl Livvy does look gorgeous."

"Alright," I chimed in, not allowing this to go much further. "If you're both done peeing on me, I think it's time to go greet our arriving guests."

Beau chuckled. "All in good fun, Elizabeth. You know how much Ethan and I enjoy busting each other's balls. Besides, you have two men battling for your affection. Ethan may claim your past, darling, but we all know I have your future."

"Claiming her past isn't the only thing that's mine forever."

"Ethan," I snapped.

Beau didn't hesitate, snapping, "What do you mean by that?"

"I mean." Ethan stepped toward him, getting close to his face. "She was my first, and don't you ever fucking forget that, Beau Hunter."

With a calm, cool demeanor, Beau didn't miss a beat. "You're right. She was. But at the end of the day, I'll be her last, Ethan Carter. Now, if you'll excuse us, my fiancée and I have an engagement party to attend."

With that, Beau grabbed my hand and led me out of the bridal suite, and I couldn't for the life of me stop looking back at Ethan as he stood there cemented in place with our past very much…

Alive and present.

ETHAN

I love her.

I stood there, debating if I was truly going to allow her to go through with this. I finally managed to pull myself together enough to walk through the doors and into her future through the walls of an ancient castle. The second I walked inside, I saw her, stopping dead in my tracks just to take her in again.

She was a vision.

There was no beauty in this world quite like Livvy Collins.

Except she was wrapped around her fiancé. She looked breathtaking, smiling at everyone. Blinding them with the millions in jewelry she was wearing on her body. I could see the diamond on her ring finger from clear across the room as if it was a fucking flashlight.

I couldn't take my eyes off her, and it took everything inside me not to make a scene. I couldn't control the internal battle that surfaced in the forefront of my mind. It was a whirlwind of emotions. Livvy would eternally own every part of me. My heart was hers since before I knew what her having it even meant. She suddenly looked down at the ground as if she felt me. The look on her face exposed the girl I grew up with, the same girl who couldn't hide her emotions from me.

Her face frowned.

Her mouth parted.

Then she stared right at me.

There was no wandering in her gaze as she found mine from the corner of the room. We looked at one another like there was no one else with us in the massive ballroom of this castle. I didn't care if anyone saw us. She placed her hand on her heart, almost like she was trying to hold it together.

My feet moved of their own accord as I followed her out onto the balcony. Once I stood behind her, I set my hands on the railing in front of her and on either side of her body. Quickly inhaling her sweet honey scent made my cock twitch. Bringing me right back to the first time I kissed her to get her to shut up when she yelled at me.

"Ethan, please..."

Slowly, I slid the tip of my fingers down her naked back, right along her exposed spine before I spun her to face me, and she immediately shut her eyes.

Leaning in, I murmured close to her mouth, "Okay, but only because you asked so nicely."

I kissed the corner of her lips, softly kissing the only spot that wasn't crossing the line. Although, a line was never drawn between us.

She belonged to me.

Plain and simple.

"Where's my necklace," I questioned, needing to know.

Since I gave it to her all those years ago, this was the first time I hadn't seen her wearing it.

"Ethan..."

"Did Beau make you take it off?"

Our emotions were running wild, trying to surrender to the connection in our souls that would always be there. I fought a battle I knew I'd never win. The emotional turmoil ate away at me. The second she felt my mouth on her skin, she opened her eyes and locked them with mine.

"What are you doing?" she let out, changing the subject.

"I'm just congratulating you on your engagement. All I want is for you to be happy, Livvy, and if Beau makes you happy, then that's all that matters to me. I'm here for you, and I'm not going anywhere. As your man of honor and as your best friend."

She breathed a sigh of relief. "Thank you, Ethan."

"I'd do anything for you."

It was the wholehearted truth. Right then and there, I knew what I had to do. I wouldn't stop the wedding. If I did, I could lose her in the process, and there wasn't a chance in hell I'd risk that. Instead, I had to make her realize she was making a mistake.

First, I'd start with...

Proving to her she really was just a trophy to him.

Chapter Twenty-One
LIVVY

To keep up appearances, our parents wanted us to sleep in separate rooms even though we already lived together. Beau's bedroom suite was literally on the other wing of the castle from mine. My suite was attached to the bridal room, and at first, I was freaked out to be sleeping by myself in this big-ass estate. This place was old as hell, making all sorts of questionable noises throughout the day.

My mother must have sensed my apprehension. While I got ready for bed after our engagement party, she came into my room to kiss me good night.

As she left, she turned and abruptly announced, "Don't worry, honey. I made sure to have Ethan's suite right next to yours. Your best friend isn't far if you need him."

The loud knock on my door the following morning sounded like a bulldozer plowing through my room. I shot straight up off the mattress, dazed and confused about where I was for a second.

"Come in," I shouted, and it echoed along the concrete walls.

Moments later, my mother walked in with Ethan behind her.

"Look at you, sleepyhead," she greeted.

I grabbed my face, rubbing sleep from my eyes. "What time is it?"

"Seven thirty."

"Mom," I bit, shaking my head. "We went to bed at almost three in the morning. Why are we awake right now?"

She smiled before making her way into the closet. "Honey," she exclaimed from inside the closet. "Your gowns will be here at eleven, and you need to get ready. Then we have breakfast scheduled at nine with your bridal party, mother-in-law, and some of Beau's family. It's all women." She stepped out of the closet. "Other than Ethan of course." She smirked at him. "Since you're Livvy's man of honor, you're one of the girls this week."

Ethan stood by the door, leaning against it with his arms crossed over his chest and one foot over the other. An amused expression spread across his face.

"I mean," Mom added, "unless you want to join the men. I'm sure Beau wouldn't mind."

"I'd mind," he stated, looking at me. "I'm here for Livvy. If that means I have to spend the rest of the week with the most beautiful women in France, then so be it."

"Ethan." Mom giggled like a schoolgirl.

I rolled my eyes, slightly chuckling. He always knew how to charm her. "Lovely," I muttered under my breath as my eyes shifted back to my mom holding a white maxi dress I bought in Europe one summer and never wore before.

"This dress will be perfect for today," she declared.

"Mom," I stressed, unpleased. "Are you planning on dressing me for the rest of the week?"

"I just want you to look your best."

"Are you saying I can't look my best if I dress myself?"

"Honey, no." She walked over to me. "I'm just saying this is such a special week, and you need to look extra put together."

I reached for the dress. "Whatever."

She handed it to me. "I also told the makeup artist to go light on your makeup. We don't want you to stain any of the wedding gowns."

"Mom, can you get some coffee before you start ordering me around, please?"

"Ethan already has that for you."

Only then did I notice a cup of coffee on the dresser. I smiled, nodding for him to bring it to me. He understood my silent command and did.

"Okay," Mom coaxed, bringing our attention back to her. "Up and at 'em, honey. The hairstylist and makeup artist will be here shortly, and we don't want to keep them waiting."

"Why do I have to get glammed right now?"

"Sweetheart." She stared at me with wide eyes. "The videographer and photographer are capturing every moment. Don't you want to look back on these precious memories and know you looked your best?"

"You keep saying that, but I didn't know I didn't look my best without a glam squad."

Ethan handed me my coffee. "You may as well get used to it, Livvy. After you're the new Mrs. Hunter, I'm sure you'll have a fleet of people around you in your new mansion."

I jerked back. "My new what?"

Ethan shrugged. "I figured you'd be moving into one of the Hunters' estates."

"Oh... yeah... that's probably what we'll do."

"You haven't spoken to him about it?"

"Not yet."

"Isn't that a discussion you should have before you get married?"

Why haven't we talked about it? If we haven't talked about that... what else haven't we discussed?

Ethan knew me like the back of his hand. I didn't have to answer his question for him to understand what I was thinking and contemplating in my mind.

Mom suggested, "I'm hoping you two choose their property in Charleston so you can finally move back home near your family."

I swallowed hard. I hadn't given any thought to us moving, let alone into a mansion that wasn't mine.

"Mom—"

"I know! I know! You're Miss Independent, but you're getting married. It's not only about you anymore. And once you have kids, I can help you if I'm close by."

"Mom, I don't know when we're having kids."

"You haven't spoken about that either?" Ethan questioned.

I opened my mouth to respond, but Mom interrupted, "Beau told us you're planning to have babies immediately."

"He said that to you?"

"Yes, he was telling everyone that last night. He's so excited to be a father. Can you imagine a little boy? Beau Prescott Hunter III. Oh! I'm so excited to be a grandma!"

I arched an eyebrow. "The third?"

"Beau's the second. What else would you name your first son?"

"Maybe something that isn't so much pressure to step into? Something that gives him more individuality perhaps?"

"You can do that with your second son, honey."

"Second? We haven't had one, and we're already discussing the second baby?"

"Elizabeth, what is with the tone?"

Ethan didn't say a word. His expression was neutral, and I couldn't read him at all. I hated when he did that. It was always much easier for him to hide his emotions from me, and now it seemed like it was his superpower.

"I just feel as if my whole future is planned out for me, and I have no say in it."

"That's not true. You know we've always wanted what's best for you, and you're marrying a Hunter, darling. Things will be expected of you. I'm sure you know that."

"Expected? Like that?"

She must have sensed my apprehension. "You know what? There's no reason we need to discuss all this right now. This week is just about you and Beau's love. Everything else will fall into place."

Will it? What things will Beau expect? And why hasn't he told me any of this?

"But, Ethan." Mom wrapped her arm around his shoulders. "Wouldn't it be amazing to have our girl move back home with us?"

"If that's what Livvy wants."

My heart fluttered. He always thought about my feelings, no matter what.

"You're right," Mom agreed. "But maybe you can persuade her." She winked at him before she left to get the glam squad.

I fell back onto the bed. "She's driving me insane, and it's only the second day of this circus."

"That's an interesting word to describe what's supposed to be the happiest week of your life."

"You know what I mean, Ethan."

"Do you know what you mean, Livvy?"

Do I?

"You better hurry up and get dressed. I saw your mother-in-law making her way over here earlier."

I peered over at him. "How long have you been up?"

"A few hours. I had to get some work done."

"Did you even sleep?"

"I don't need much sleep these days."

"All work and no play makes Ethan a dull boy. You said you could take the week off for me."

He held his hands out in front of him. "And here I am."

"Are you going to be sneak-working the entire time?"

"Not the entire time."

"Ethan…"

Chapter Twenty-Two
LIVVY

"Don't worry about me. I'm here for you regardless."

I smiled wide. "And I'm so grateful for that. You'll help me keep my sanity from my parents."

"They just want what's best for you."

"You always agree with them."

"I'm not agreeing. I'm simply stating a fact."

"Yeah, but—"

"I wasn't raised by my parents." He'd never mentioned anything like that. I was rendered speechless when he spoke with conviction...

"I have a much different perspective on family than you."

Feeling ballsy, I asked, "Have you seen or spoken to your father?"

"To hell with my father, Livvy."

I frowned. "Is that a yes?"

He changed the subject. "Who's in your bridal party?"

I reluctantly sighed, giving up. This was the only topic he would never discuss with me. Not once.

Instead of putting up a fight for more information, I smiled. Fully aware he knew I didn't have many girlfriends to count on. "Two college friends and like five hundred cousins."

He nodded, stepping back. "I'm going to let you get dressed. I'll see you at breakfast. I'll be the one cock at the table."

I laughed, waving goodbye.

For the rest of the morning, I was thrown around like a rag doll. From one seat to another, I could barely keep up with the endless questions thrown my way from everyone.

"How many kids do you plan on having?"

"Where are you going to live?"

"What names have you decided for your kids?"

"Are you planning on private schools?"

"Do you know what religion you'll be raising them?"

At one point, I swear the room began spinning, especially after I started trying on my wedding gowns.

"All of these are stunning," I remarked. "How am I going to choose one?"

Mrs. Hunter replied, "I'm glad these impress you, Elizabeth." She looked as glamorous as always, wearing a beige dress.

"Wow! I don't even know what to say. This is so unreal. I've never been in anything like this," I revealed, staring at myself wearing a Valentino mermaid gown in the floor-length mirror in front of me.

They turned the sitting room in the castle into my very own bridal shop. Gown after gown hung on racks across the room.

Every style.

Every fabric.

Every designer.

Nothing cost less than twenty thousand dollars. A few of the dresses were over a hundred.

Everyone decided I needed three different options. One for the ceremony, one for the introduction, our first dance, and dinner, and then the last one for the party. Our wedding started at six in the evening and didn't end until the wee hours of the morning. They also agreed that I had to have three different hairstyles for each one. I'd spend a good portion of the night just changing and getting my hair done like I was Malibu Barbie, the redheaded version.

"Well, get used to it, my precious daughter-in-law." Mrs. Hunter grabbed my hand, turning me around. "I mean, look at you. You're radiant. You're a vision. A one of a kind. From your long, natural red hair to your bright green eyes that my son loves so much. Your freckles are youthful and adorable, and your makeup is absolutely flawless. You remind me of a pretty princess, and every princess deserves glamour, gold, and diamonds."

Beau's mother was always lovely to me, and she obviously worshipped her son. However, she was your typical Stepford trophy wife, but she genuinely seemed happy in that role. Mr. Hunter was attentive, caring, and very loving toward her. It appeared as if they were happily married, and Beau never told me otherwise.

"You and Beau will make gorgeous babies. I can't wait for you to make me a grandmother. You'll hire the same nanny I had for Hunter. You'll use the same OB-GYN. Oh my goodness! I'm so excited for baby Beau."

Nanny? OB-GYN? Baby Beau? What. The. Fuck?

If the room wasn't spinning before, now it was sideways.

"With all due respect, I don't want a nanny raising my kids, Mrs. Hunter."

"Oh, don't be silly, darling. You'll always be the mother, but you'll need help with five children. Especially after you quit your job and become a stay-at-home mom and wife. Your job will be taking care of your family."

"Wait, what?"

"Yes, Beau always wanted a big family. Unfortunately, I wasn't blessed with any more than Beau, but he was so perfect, I never felt the loss of not having more children."

It was like I was in this alternate universe. If I thought my parents didn't listen to me, his would be far worse.

"Now this..." Mrs. Hunter grabbed another gown off one of the gold racks. "This... is what dreams are made of."

I was officially in couture hell, and as I stared at myself in the mirror, I didn't recognize the woman staring back at me. She was a complete stranger. Not even a version of myself, but a whole-ass other person.

Shouldn't I recognize myself in my own wedding gown? Wasn't it the point to look like myself?

Shaking off the endless questions, I stepped off the stage they made for me and asked the butler for a glass of wine.

"Martello, please make sure it's white wine," Mom added, making me feel even worse if that was possible. "The last thing we need is a red stain on the dress."

For the rest of the fitting, I thought about nothing and everything as I looked into that mirror. My heart beat a mile a minute. I couldn't help but watch my mother-in-law's demeanor.

Her mannerisms.

Her composure.

The way she spoke—always prim and proper.

Everything about her screamed perfection.

Her hair.

Her nails.

Her makeup and outfit.

Will Beau expect me to be like her?

My thoughts raced as much as my pulse was.

I bit my bottom lip, a nervous habit I developed in childhood. All of a sudden, I saw Ethan leaning against the far wall as if he appeared out of thin air.

He mouthed, "Stop biting your lip."

It immediately threw me back to another place and time where I was hanging on his back before he hung us on the rope to jump into our waterhole. It was right before he kissed me for the first time.

He grinned like he knew what I envisioned.

We stared at each other through the mirror, the same way Beau and I had the night prior. There in front of me was my future in a wedding gown while behind me stood my past where no one could see him except for me...

And the irony was not lost on me.

ETHAN

Once again, I couldn't take my eyes off her, and I didn't want to until my cell phone vibrated in the pocket of my black slacks.

I answered, "This is Ethan."

No one could hear me. I stood in a secluded corner of the room, watching Livvy try on her wedding gowns. The way they threw her around all morning was quite a sight to see. Especially watching her mumble her answers to questions you'd think she and Beau had already communicated, but it was obvious they hadn't.

What kind of relationship is that?

"Good afternoon, Ethan," my lawyer greeted.

"Any updates?"

"We're still trying to find whatever we can on Beau Hunter. I was just calling to ask if you want us to continue now that you're at their wedding."

Freddie had been with me since I began my app. There wasn't much I kept from him. He knew my situation with Livvy, and I appreciated his sentiment, making sure I was doing the right thing.

Still locking eyes with Livvy through the mirror, I had no problem confirming...

"Abso-fucking-lutely."

Chapter Twenty-Three
LIVVY

Early the following morning, it was our third day into our weeklong wedding celebration, and I found myself walking into Beau's suite before they left to go golfing again. After they returned yesterday, I didn't get a moment alone with him, and by the time I did, it was late into the night, and I didn't want to bring it up anymore.

I should have, though. I barely slept, tossing and turning most of the night, thinking about all the questions that plagued me. As soon as I walked into his west wing suite, Beau was walking out of the bathroom with a white towel wrapped around his waist. His sculpted physique was messing with my head, and I had to shake off the desire to have sex with him instead.

"You're up early," he announced, kissing me.

I smiled, peering up at him. He was so tall, almost the same height as Ethan who was six-foot-three. However, Beau's appearance was totally opposite from Ethan's. He had blond hair, green eyes, and kind of resembled a version of the Ken doll. He was definitely a pretty boy as opposed to Ethan, who looked more rugged. They were both devastatingly handsome, and women constantly stared at them everywhere we went.

"I wanted to catch you before you left," I expressed. "Once you return, you know we won't have a second alone together."

He smacked my ass, causing me to yelp. "I like where this is going." In one swift movement, he wrapped my legs around his waist and carried me over to the bed. "God, I've missed you."

"Beau, this isn't—"

Throwing me onto the bed, he laid perfectly on top of me as he held himself up by his arms on the sides of my head, caging me in.

"Well." He kissed my neck. "Allow me to change your mind."

"I'm being serious. We need to talk."

"We can still talk." He nuzzled his way down my chest. "I'm listening to every word you say."

I grabbed his chin to look at me. "I can't focus when you're doing that."

He chuckled, vibrating my entire core.

"Then all the more reason for me to keep going."

"Please..."

"Alright." He paused, giving me his attention. "What's wrong?"

"Nothing's wrong."

"It doesn't look like nothing's wrong."

"I just want to talk about some things, that's all."

"What things?"

"Okay..." Inhaling a deep breath, I questioned, "Beau, are we moving into one of your parents' estates?"

"Not unless you don't want to."

"Are you sure about that?"

"What are you expecting me to say?"

"I'm not sure." I shrugged. "Why didn't you tell me that was a possibility to begin with?"

"It has no relevancy to us now."

"We're getting married in four days. Isn't this something we should have talked about before?"

"We're talking about it right now."

"Only because I brought it up."

He cocked his head to the side. "Did my mother say something to you to bring this on?"

"No," I firmly stated. "My mother did. She's expecting us to move into your family's Charleston property."

"I'm not seeing the issue. Don't you want to be closer to your parents? Ethan?"

"I do, but I also have a very important job to think about. You're talking about uprooting my entire life."

"Sweetheart, you could open your own law practice. You don't need to work for anyone else."

My eyes widened. "Sounds like you've already given this some thought?"

"Not any more than you have." He sat back on his legs. "I just assumed you'd love nothing more than to move back to your childhood state. Other than your job, what else is keeping you in California?"

"I'm not saying you're wrong. I just don't like to be blindsided by my mom of all people. If the roles were reversed, I'm almost positive you wouldn't appreciate it either."

By the serious expression on his face, he was considering it. "You're right. I wouldn't."

"Okay... so what is this that I'm hearing you're basically trying to knock me up on our honeymoon?"

"I'm not going to pretend I'm not excited to have a family with you."

"Don't you think we need to talk about that first?"

"I imagine we would after we were married."

"Again," I stressed. "Isn't that something we should discuss before we walk down the aisle? Because I'd like to be married for a little bit before we go down that road."

"Elizabeth, we've been on and off for the past ten years. How much more time do you need?"

"You say it like it's a bad thing?"

"Sweetheart." He lovingly smiled at me. "Why don't you just get off the pill, and we can leave it up to fate to see what happens?"

"Getting off the pill is not fate, Beau. That's preparing."

"Is this about you gaining weight while you're pregnant?"

"Of course not." I sat up, offended. "Why would you even think that?"

"I thought most women's fear was that their husbands wouldn't find them attractive while they're pregnant, but let me reassure you, I can't wait to see your stomach rounded by my son."

"Your son?" I frowned. "What if it's a girl?"

"Well, let's hope it's not."

I shook my head, not understanding. "What's wrong with a girl?"

"Nothing is wrong with a little girl, and I can't wait to have one with you, but a baby girl needs an older brother to protect her. Besides, we need to begin our patriarchy with a son."

"Our patriarchy? What in the fuck does that mean?"

"Livvy..."

"Don't call me that. Why are you calling me that? You never call me that."

"Why can't I? Or does that nickname only belong to Ethan?"

I jerked back, suddenly annoyed. "Are you really trying to pull this again? I thought we were long past this?"

"Elizabeth." He grabbed my hand. "I'm sorry. You're right. We're long past this." It was obvious he was weighing his words. "I was just... I mean, *we were just* raised in very patriarchal families. It's what we both know. I assumed—"

"You're assuming a lot. Are you saying you expect me to quit my job and be Suzy Homemaker?"

"If you don't want to quit your job, then it's your choice. I'm not trying to marry my mother. I love you for the strong, independent woman that you are."

"Do you mean that?"

"I wouldn't be saying it to you if I didn't mean it. Darling, I'm sorry that our parents are getting to you, but in regard to our future, it's *our* future. Not theirs. I love you very much, and from here on out, we will make our choices together without worrying about what anyone else thinks. If you want to stay in California, we can. If you don't want to move into any of my family's estates, then so be it. I don't care. None of that matters to me. The only thing that matters to me is you and you becoming my wife."

I threw my arms around his neck, feeling like a massive weight had been lifted off my shoulders. "Thank God! You have no idea how much

I've been freaking out. Between my parents and yours and all our guests and family... I'm ready to lose my mind, and it's only the third day. I can't keep up with the relentless questions of all the things we haven't discussed, and it's freaking me the fuck out."

He laughed, rubbing my back in a comforting gesture. "Sweetheart, this is me and you. We will decide what's best for our future. Don't let them get to you."

"I'll try. I'm just... I don't know... I just wasn't expecting anything like this. It's a lot to take in. We're basically having a royal wedding at this point."

"We both come from powerful, wealthy families. What else did you expect?"

"Well for starters, I didn't think we'd be in separate bedrooms."

"I know." He nodded, rubbing my neck with his mouth. "But it'll be over soon, and we can put this behind us and start our future together the way we want. Not the way anyone expects us to."

I held him tighter. "Do you promise?"

"Of course." He pulled away, grabbing my face. "Do you feel better now?"

"Yes."

"Good." He kissed me.

"You're so lucky, Beau. You don't have to deal with all the women and all the things they have planned for me. You just get to golf, smoke cigars, and drink. If it weren't for Ethan, I would have gone crazy already."

"In that case, let me show you how sorry I am." Moving forward, he laid me down on the mattress again. "I'm so lucky. How did I get this lucky to have you?"

I smiled, enjoying his undivided attention.

"I'm waiting on my sorry."

He chuckled. "You don't have to tell me twice." Slowly, he pecked his way down my torso when all of a sudden, there was a knock on his door.

Beau shouted, "I'm getting ready. I'll be out in twenty minutes."

I giggled. "Liar."

"Shhh," he playfully ordered, lightly biting my bottom lip.

I was surprised when I heard Ethan's voice come through the door. "Is Livvy in there with you? Her mother is looking for her."

I remarked, "I guess this is to be continued?"

Beau growled with an irritated expression. After he got off me, I thought he would go into the bathroom, but instead, he answered the door. He opened it wide so Ethan realized what he was interrupting.

Ethan took one look at him and then back at me before he cleared his throat and bowed his head.

"By all means," Beau baited, seeing his discomfort. "I was just spending some quality time inside my fiancée."

"Beau!" I reprimanded, shaking my head in disappointment.

"I can't imagine much quality time can be spent in five minutes?" Ethan elaborated. "But I guess Livvy's used to your lack of stamina."

"Okay!" I jumped out of bed, hurrying between them. Closing my robe tighter, I demanded, "On that note. We can go."

The last thing I needed was another pissing contest over who I belonged to more. I kissed Beau and quickly grabbed Ethan by his arm, basically dragging him out of there.

Once we were out of earshot, I acknowledged, "Just for the record, there was no quality time inside me for five minutes."

Ethan mischievously smiled, wrapping his arm around my shoulders as we walked back to our suites on the other side of the castle.

"Don't worry, Livvy. I knew that'd be too long for good ole Beau."

I rolled my eyes. "Are you two ever going to get along? You're like two rabid dogs constantly fighting over me like I'm nothing more than a juicy bone."

"You're so much more than just a bone, Livvy. You're the whole damn five-star course meal."

"Charmer," I teased, patting him on the chest. "Now I have to spend hours getting ready for the bridal luncheon today that I'm dreading already."

"What's left on the itinerary after today?"

"Let's see." I thought about it. "Tomorrow is Thursday, which is the fourth day, so that would make it the bridal party, but I don't know why it's even called that since Beau, his friends, and everyone else is attending. I think it's just a way of having another party and calling it something different. Then Friday we have the bridal shower, Saturday we have bachelor and bachelorette parties, and Sunday is the big day with the ceremony and wedding."

"What time is the bridal shower tomorrow?"

"Noon to three."

"Alright, after it's over." He glanced at me, and in a stern tone, he noted, "You're mine."

I smiled wide. "I think I could make that happen. Oh! That reminds me, why was my mom looking for me?"

With yet another mischievous smirk, Ethan admitted...

"Your mom was looking for you?"

Chapter Twenty-Four

ETHAN

The last day and a half seemed as if it were a blur. If I had to listen to Livvy receiving marriage advice one more time, I was going to lose my shit. Half these women wouldn't know a good marriage if it bit them in the ass.

I walked into the banquet hall for the bridal party with a drink in my hand, immediately running into Livvy's old man.

"Ethan," Mr. Collins greeted, shaking my hand. "How have you been holding up with the women every day? I told Livvy that you're more than welcome to join us, but she was adamant that you were fine with her."

"I am, sir, but thanks for the invitation."

"You're a good man." He gripped my shoulder. "I'm sure you've heard all the wives complain about their husbands, so tell me, how did I hold up with Mrs. Collins?"

I chuckled. "Not too bad."

"That's great to hear." He clinked his drink with mine. "How's business? I feel like I haven't had a moment alone with you to congratulate you on all your success. I've been following your career since the beginning, and from one entrepreneur man to another, I'm damn impressed with everything you've accomplished in just four years."

I never expected him to say that to me, and I was a bit thrown off.

He scoffed out, "I know. I know. I haven't always been a fan of yours through the years, but you really did prove yourself to me when you let Livvy go. I'll forever be grateful for you allowing my baby girl to find her independence. And look at her now, an attorney at a top law firm in California and marrying a Hunter. I couldn't be prouder."

"Yeah, well, appearances can be deceiving, sir."

He narrowed his eyes at me. "Are you talking about Beau? You don't approve?"

I shrugged. "It doesn't matter what I think. All that matters is that our girl's happy."

"Ethan, if you know something about Beau—"

"What about me?" Beau chimed in, walking up beside Mr. Collins with Livvy on his arm.

"Oh, I need to take this call," Mr. Collins announced, grabbing his phone as he walked away.

"I was just telling Mr. Collins that appearances can be deceiving."

"I couldn't agree more." Beau indicated, "Starting with the woman who is eye fucking the shit out of you, Ethan."

My gaze shifted to see Varissa making her way over to me.

Fuck.

"Ethan." She beamed once she stood in front of me. "Now, this is the last place I'd think to run into you." She leaned in, kissing my left cheek and then my right.

"You two know each other?" Beau asked, peering back and forth between us.

Livvy answered, "I think everybody knows who she is, Beau."

"Oh, stop..." Varissa waved her off, but deep down, she loved the compliment.

She was a supermodel, after all.

Within seconds, several people crowded around her, asking to take a picture with her while Beau tended to the guests who were suddenly surrounding them too.

I backed away, walking to the bar instead. I needed another drink. After I tipped the bartender, I ended up on the balcony Livvy and I were standing on the night of their engagement/welcome party.

It wasn't long until I was aware that Livvy stood behind me. I could feel her from anywhere in the room. However, I waited for her to make her presence known, mindful that this wouldn't be a pleasant conversation.

Our profound connection to each other was strong at that moment. On nights like these, I'd look up at the night sky, wondering whether Livvy stared up at them with me miles away. I often thought about if things would be different if she had stayed in Charleston and didn't move to California.

I thought about our pregnancy scare or even worse...

If she had actually been pregnant.

Hundreds of questions consumed my thoughts, whether I was awake or asleep.

All I ever wanted was to do right by her. Even if I hurt myself in the process. One thing that did change in me after she left was that I never gave my heart to another woman.

I never opened up to anyone else.

I never let anyone in.

There were no girlfriends.

No dating.

No relationships in that way.

Not when Livvy owned every last part of me. She was my beginning and end. She would forever be a part of me, even when she was in the arms of her fiancé.

The motherfucker I hated so damn much, and still, I didn't have any incriminating evidence on him yet. The days were coming to an end, and soon, I wouldn't have any time left.

Livvy broke my train of thought, sarcastically asking, "Are you planning on having a private yacht, work trip with Varissa in your suite?"

Unable to hold back, I turned with my arms on the railing. "You sound jealous?"

She adamantly shook her head. "I'm not. But you'd think that attending someone else's bridal party, you wouldn't wear a skimpy dress that barely covers your body."

"I hadn't noticed. I was too busy looking at what you were wearing."

Eyeing her up and down, I admired her fitted white strapless gown that was low cut in the front. Simply accentuating each and every delicious curve of her irresistible body with a high slit that came up on her right thigh. Her hair flowed loosely in large curls, framing her face. I couldn't help but notice every feature, especially her pouty red lips.

"She's captured the attention of every man in the room."

"Yeah, including your fiancé's."

She glared at me.

"Shouldn't you be riding Beau's ass and not mine?"

She ignored my question. "Did you invite her here?"

"Does it look like I invited her?"

"Then why is she here?"

"Your guess is as good as mine, but this is a high-society celebration. She's probably on the guest list to bring more attention to your big day."

Livvy didn't try to hide her jealousy, and I'd be lying if I said I wasn't loving every second of it.

"How many times have you been with her?"

"Too many to count." I pushed off the wall, purposely striding over to her.

After all these years, her bright green eyes still had the power to bring me to my knees with a simple look or smile. Something in her stare told me she wanted to express so much. There she was, my girl, lost in her thoughts as I candidly desired her.

Her smell.

Her touch.

Her taste.

Craving her.

Needing her.

Wanting her in every possible way.

Possessiveness washed over me at a rapid speed, spreading clear across the small distance between us.

"There you are, Ethan," Varissa interrupted, stopping me dead in my tracks.

"I've been looking all over for you." She spun to Livvy. "Can I just tell you that you're going to make such a gorgeous bride? Your fiancé won't stop talking about you. I hope to find a love like that one day, but who knows... maybe your wedding will bring me luck." As if on cue, Varissa locked eyes with me. "I'd love to catch the bouquet."

"There's my gorgeous bride," Beau exclaimed, reaching for her hand. "Mr. Charlesworth wants to meet you." He nodded to Varissa and me. "If you'll excuse us."

After they were gone, Varissa smirked. "Dance with me."

I simply nodded, and she grabbed my hand, leading me to the dance floor before I wrapped my arm around her lower back. She placed her left hand on my shoulder, and we entwined our other hands at our sides.

Varissa didn't hesitate to set her leg between mine, so she was straddling my thigh.

She allowed no distance between us, purring in my ear, "I've missed you so much, Ethan."

When Livvy came into sight, she was already glaring daggers in our direction. As always, her fiancé was oblivious to her, paying more attention to whoever's ass he was kissing. I could physically feel Livvy's restraint being stretched to the max. Her collected composure cracked momentarily as her eyes turned murderous, her nostrils flaring for a split second.

It only confirmed what I already knew.

She still fucking loved me.

Heart.

Body.

Soul.

I continued to dance with Varissa while Livvy's fiery stare burned into my skin.

Nothing could have prepared me for her reaction.

Chapter Twenty-Five

ETHAN

She knew damn well she was the only woman who always faithfully had my attention and devotion.

After the song was over, Varissa went to the bathroom, and I asked Livvy to dance. Despite being pissed for no reason whatsoever, she agreed. The last thing she wanted to do was make a scene, and that was exactly what would happen if she hauled ass away from me.

I hooked my arm around her lower back, placing her right hand into my left at our sides, and proceeded to dance with her.

"Are you two going to have a sleepover tonight?"

"Why does it matter?"

"Because my room is next to yours, and she seems like a screamer." She pushed off my chest a little too hard into a turn, spinning back into our hold.

"She's not any louder than you were."

Her lips parted, and I affectionately moved my right hand to the back of her neck as we started to dance effortlessly around the room like we were the only two people in the space. To an outsider looking in, we were simply two childhood best friends fondly dancing together.

"Whatever," Livvy snapped, playing it off like I wasn't on to her.

The violins from the orchestra hit a high point in the ballad, and I wrapped her left arm around my neck. We gazed deep into each other's eyes, and the intensity of the music took over, only adding to the craze of our heated expression.

It was filled with so much intensity I could barely take it, and I had to remind her…

"Livvy, you're forever my girl."

LIVVY

I blinked, and I was suddenly standing back on that balcony. The orchestra continue to play in the distance from inside. I couldn't remember the last time I just stood still, appreciating the scenic view for what felt like the first time.

The escape I sought was nowhere to be found under the full moon, dancing off the castle. Only darkness surrounded me like the sadness reflecting off my heart at the moment. I watched the wind blow the trees for I don't know how long, letting my mind wander to a time when things weren't so fucking complicated.

I love Beau, but why did I feel as if I wanted to burn the whole place down because they're dancing?

I didn't know how Ethan was still able to elicit emotions I thought were long buried. It wasn't him dancing with the supermodel that bothered me the most. It was that I wanted to be the woman he was dancing with and not her.

Watching Ethan these past few days was quite a sight.

The power he exuded.

The way he governed any room.

Ethan Carter truly turned into the man my father always wanted me to marry. He was a Beau Hunter in his own right, becoming a self-made billionaire instead of born with a silver spoon in his mouth like my fiancé and I were.

I stayed there for I don't know how long when I unexpectedly felt Ethan behind me. Except I couldn't turn to face him at that moment. It was too difficult. The overwhelming emotions were too heavy to endure, and I knew he could see right through them.

He could see right through me.

In ways Beau didn't.

Couldn't.

Shaking off the unrelenting feelings that Ethan evoked from deep within my body, I opened my mouth to say something.

Anything.

But there was only silence.

He was the first to close the distance between us. Merely adding to the internal battle that surfaced in the forefront of my mind. It was a whirlwind of thoughts racing profusely.

From my mind.

To my heart.

To every bone in my body.

I looked down at the ground when his looming presence behind me was too much to bear. My breathing hitched, but I stayed firmly in the place I was standing.

I didn't move; cemented in place.

It seemed like I was barely breathing.

It was a moment where I felt completely vulnerable and exposed, making it easy to share the only thing I could…

"I still think about that summer. From prom night to our last goodbye. It haunts me, Ethan. Is that what you want to know?" I could feel the tears rimming my eyes. "I moved away because I thought it would be easier for the both of us. Our friendship was too important to ever sacrifice that with having a real relationship with you. However, that didn't take away the love I felt for you. The love I still feel for you." I paused, clearing my throat to stop my emotions from getting the best of me. "As much as we swore what happened between us wouldn't change our friendship, it did. You were all I had, and then I was alone and found Beau. For years, a little part of me felt like I was trying to replace that love I felt for you with him."

I protectively wrapped my arms around my stomach in a comforting gesture, desperately trying to hold in the memories that threatened to spill. Thinking about the past and the future, I closed my eyes, and although we weren't touching, I felt him all over.

There was no hiding…

From him.

From me.

From us.

It physically pained me to stand there with him, telling him everything I didn't want him to know until I finally spun to face him. His expression mirrored mine, almost rendering me speechless.

"I do love Beau, Ethan. But for a long time, he was right. I did put you before him, before everything. Though somewhere along the way... I did fall in love with him."

He winced, and I hated that I was hurting him.

"I have no right to get jealous of you with any woman. You're not mine. You never were. I'm getting married, for God's sake. I have no business involving myself in yours. You're free to be with anyone you want, and it's shameful that I'm getting riled up over my best friend possibly finding a love of his own. It's selfish and unfair to you, and I'm ashamed for even feeling this way and for making you feel bad about being with someone you've obviously hooked up with for who knows how long."

"That's where you're wrong, Livvy. I'll always be yours, and you'll always be mine."

"I'm getting married in three days, Ethan. I'm going to be someone's wife, to have and to hold, in sickness and in health, till death do us part. I'm going to be the mother of his children—he's going to be the father of mine. You can't say stuff like that to me anymore. It's not right."

"Everything about us is right."

"Enough!" I shouted a little too loudly, but the loud orchestra muffled my tone.

I didn't want to make a scene or draw any unnecessary attention to us. Especially with my fiancé. Beau didn't deserve any of this, and I had to put a stop to it. I should have done it a long time ago, but this was the first time in years that I'd seen Ethan with another woman.

It hurt me in ways I hadn't expected and only made me feel that much worse. I wasn't this girl. I was committed to Beau, and I had to prove that to myself.

I was his.

Only his.

In order to officially put our past behind me, our summer and everything between, I did what I had to do. Fisting my hands, I fought with the words that already tasted like battery acid on my tongue and I hadn't even said them yet. Merely thinking about them crippled my apprehension not to want to say them at all.

You have to do this, Livvy. You owe it to your husband-to-be.

In a determined tone, I declared, "You'll forever be my best friend, but I can't keep putting you up on a pedestal before him anymore."

"Livvy—"

"I know I promised you that I'd never forget that I was yours first."

His eyes widened with so much emotion it almost knocked me on my ass.

"I'm so sorry, Ethan."

I had to be strong. In spite of regretting the words as soon as they left my mouth, I clearly stated, "I should have never made that promise to you."

"Is that why you stopped wearing my necklace?"

I couldn't lie to him.

I never could.

I hated this.

In one word, I killed us both...

"Yes."

Chapter Twenty-Six
LIVVY

Ethan disappeared after I left him on the balcony by himself. I didn't see him for the rest of the night, and to make matters worse, I didn't see Varissa either. I tried to distract myself with the party, but it was useless. He was front and center on my mind regardless of how many guests I spoke to.

It didn't help that Beau noticed Varissa and Ethan were gone as well, pointing out that they were probably together. By the time I made it back to my suite, it was past three in the morning. Since the walls were made of concrete, I couldn't hear a damn thing coming out of his room.

With my hand in the air, I battled with the desire to knock on his door. Ultimately, I walked into my room without finding out the truth of what they might have been doing. I tried to pretend it didn't matter, like I didn't care, but that was impossible. The fact that I had to lay there all night with images of them fucking right in the next room was the hardest form of torture.

Which was completely and utterly ridiculous.

The next morning came far too late, and I half expected him to walk into my suite with coffee in his hand or at least come in with my mom like he had been all week.

That Friday morning, he did none of those two things. He was once again nowhere to be found, and I couldn't bring myself to knock on his door in case he was no longer there. Instead of being relieved that my bridal shower was that morning, Ethan didn't attend that either.

Since I was put on the spot, I lied to everyone that he was unexpectedly pulled into a work thing and wouldn't be joining us. The bridal shower was filled with more marriage advice I didn't care to hear and an overwhelming number of gifts to open. When it was finally over, I hurried back to my room for some time alone.

I barely slept the night before and was exhausted and emotionally drained from the entire week. Ethan and I were supposed to spend the rest of the afternoon together, but I was beginning to think he flew back to Charleston.

I changed out of my white dress, throwing on a pair of jeans and a tank top. Beau wouldn't be back for a few hours, so I was alone for the first time since we landed in France, other than when I was sleeping.

I sat in the reading nook by the window, aimlessly staring out at the garden as my thoughts sped a mile a minute until there was a knock on the door.

"I'm coming!" I announced, opening it.

My heart immediately dropped to the ground, wholeheartedly not expecting to see him.

"Ethan," I softly greeted, gazing into his serene eyes that always did things to me.

The silence between us was deafening as we just stood there, lost in each other's presence for a moment. We took one another in as if we hadn't seen each other just last night. I watched the way his lips moved with each quick breath that blew out of his mouth. I knew his heart was racing as fast as mine was.

I watched the way his hair blew in the wind from the open windows, framing his defined face and intense stare solely focused on me.

I watched the way his solid muscular chest heaved up and down, mirroring mine like they were in sync.

I especially watched the way he looked at me. It was now engrained in my mind, in my memory, in every last part of me.

When he casually brushed my hair away from my face, he still didn't say a word.

The emotion he was openly showing me was consuming...

I could touch it.

Feel it.

Taste it.

My heart fluttered, my stomach dropped again, and my mouth parted the instant he rasped, "Hi, Livvy."

I hid back a smile, unaware of how to proceed with him until I replied, "Hi, Ethan."

He never tried hiding from me. Always showed me his true colors no matter the circumstance.

What you saw was what you got.

What he said was what he meant.

Whether I wanted to see it or not.

I swallowed hard, dying to ask him if he was with Varissa.

"Come on." He nodded with a sly grin.

My eyebrows pinched together. "Where?"

"Would it matter? You're mine for the rest of the afternoon, remember? Take a ride with me. I want to show you something."

He reached for my hand and my resolve quickly shattered while I grabbed his. I tried not to get emotional while he drove us to wherever he was taking me, but it was difficult not to. An endless stream of conflicting emotions spiraled through my mind, tearing right at my heart. Confusing me even more when it came to him, but in a much different way than before.

I closed my eyes just for a second, too consumed with feelings I didn't know how to stop. I tried ignoring the looming feeling in the pit of my stomach, focusing on the beautiful scenic route he drove us on instead. My thoughts never stopped racing as I desperately tried enjoying the fresh breeze in my face. I tried living in the moment with Ethan, even if it wouldn't last. I sought the refuge he always provided, with or without him even knowing it.

Which was yet another thing about Ethan...

He wanted to see the truths that most people tried to ignore.

The way he looked at me, the way he spoke to me, the way he listened.

Every smile.

Every laugh.

Every word that fell from his lips meant something.

It didn't matter how big or small.

It was there.

Etching its way into my heart where no one could ever come close to it.

Not that I had ever let them.

Even with my fiancé.

When Ethan slowed down and took a turn onto a secluded road that read *Private Property* at the entrance, I asked, "Where are we going?"

He smiled, pulling into a makeshift parking spot in a forest. We were in the countryside, and before I knew what was happening, as if reading my mind, he tilted his head to the side, enticing me with whatever he was going to say.

I licked my lips, my mouth suddenly dry. His mischievous glare shadowed the movement of my tongue. So when he slowly stepped out of the SUV, taking his warmth with him, I followed him. Once we rounded the hood of the vehicle, he turned and grabbed my hand to lead us onto a cemented walkway. My eyes shifted swiftly from him to the surprise suddenly in front of me.

"Oh my God." There, in front of my eyes, was our own little waterhole in France.

I couldn't believe it.

"How did you find this place?"

He smiled, big and wide, and what proceeded next happened so fast that I never saw it coming. In an instant, he threw me over his shoulder like I weighed nothing and hauled ass toward the water.

"Ethan! Don't you dare!"

Of course, he didn't listen to me. Not that I expected him to. In a flash, he threw me into the stream. For the next hour, we played in the water like two young teenagers with their whole lives ahead of them.

"I can't believe you did this," I exclaimed, sitting next to him in the water to watch the sunset.

"I figured you could use some fun that doesn't involve catering to hundreds of people."

"Is that what you think I'm doing?"

"Livvy, you've always been a people pleaser. Especially when it came to your parents."

"Yeah," I said.

He was right, so there was no point arguing with him about it.

"Do you think if I wasn't marrying a Hunter, my parents would have still turned my wedding into the social event of the year? I haven't chosen one thing for this week. Is that normal? Does the bride usually not have a say in her own big day?"

He shrugged. "You're asking the wrong man. If it weren't for you, I would have grown up alone. I don't have two parents who love me like your mom and dad love you. I'm not sure of the protocol, but I'm assuming it probably also has something to do with the fact that your father has always been high profile. More so now than ever."

"Right…" Unable to hold back, I asked, "Where did you go last night after we spoke on the balcony?"

"I went back to my room and worked some until I knocked on your door."

Eyeing him up and down, I couldn't resist. "Were you with Varissa?"

"Yeah." He nodded. "I was."

That felt like a huge knife in my heart.

Don't cry, Livvy. Please don't fucking cry.

"Well, I'm glad you got to have some company in such a romantic country."

"It wasn't her company I was after."

"Yeah, okay. I don't need the details, Casanova."

"In fact, I wasn't after anything other than wanting to be alone."

"So what? You kicked her out after you had sex with her?"

"Something like that."

"That's nice of you."

"Except for one thing."

I mocked, "I can't wait to hear it."

"I kicked her out before I fucked her."

I chuckled, pretending that I wasn't relieved.

He nudged my shoulder with his. "You know millions of girls would love to trade places with you."

"I know, and I'm not trying to be ungrateful, but I can't remember a time when what I wanted mattered to my parents. You know? It's always been march in line or else."

"It could be worse. You could have had a mother you don't remember and a father who doesn't give a flying fuck about you until you're worth billions."

I turned to face him, surprised he mentioned them. "Have you talked to your dad?"

"Not recently."

"When was the last time?"

"Two years ago."

"Oh wow… you never told me that."

"There's nothing to tell other than he called me randomly one night asking for money before he even said hello."

My heart broke for him. "I'm so sorry. I can't imagine what that felt like, but you know what? Fuck him," I snapped. "Look at everything you've accomplished without him. In spite of him. You're Ethan Carter, you've been on the cover of *Forbes*, *The New York Times*, you're literally one of the richest men in the world, and you did that all on your own with no one pushing you or helping you."

"I had you," he coaxed, locking gazes with me. "You got me through it. You're not only my best friend but you're also my family. I love you, Livvy. I'll always love you."

My eyes watered as he softly brushed the hair away from my face with the back of his fingers. Music from someone's house started playing through the trees, and I stood, bringing him with me. Taking one of my hands, I placed it on his shoulder. Intertwining my other hand with his, we moved to the beat of the music while he hummed the soft melody in my ear.

You never realized how much your childhood affected the person you are. How your memories shaped your life and who you became.

All of mine included Ethan.

We spent the next hour just dancing, and I couldn't for the life of me shake off the memory of prom. And for the first time, I thought to myself…

Am I marrying the right man?

Chapter Twenty-Seven

ETHAN

I was down to my last day of finding out anything on Beau Hunter II, but so far, my team hadn't dug up one fucking thing. Tonight were the separate bachelor and bachelorette parties, and I spent most of the day working in my suite. I knew the bride and groom were spending some alone time together before the big day tomorrow, so I kept to myself in my room.

I wasn't sure what the plan was for tonight. Her bridesmaids decided to take the reins, and I was grateful for it. Though it was typically the maid of honor duties, I was the man of honor, and I had no clue what a bunch of women wanted to get into.

I sure as shit was not expecting a bunch of dicks in my face. From the cock necklaces they wore to the cock drinks they were carrying, along with a cock straw they were sucking out of and cock lollipops they were actually sucking.

Not to mention, they had a list of inappropriate tasks Livvy had to do, like ask a man for his boxers, get spanked from a group of guys, and take a photo with a tattooed bartender, just to name a few. It wasn't until we walked into a male revue that I almost turned right back around. Instead, I stood in the corner of the room, finishing up some emails while the girls lost their shit over sweaty, half-naked men.

I didn't realize women were way worse than men when it came to these things. All boundaries were checked at the door, and I tried to keep busy while they had their fun. Once they called Livvy's name through the speakers to go onto the stage, it was my turn to almost lose my shit. I resisted the urge to jump on stage and drag her out of there the second they laid her down on the floor.

For the next few minutes, I experienced what could only be described as pure and utter torture. Thank God, I could see it was all in good fun, or I would have carried her off if I felt like she was getting taken advantage of. It didn't stop the torment I felt, though.

If this was what the women were getting into, I could only imagine the men. As much as I wanted to accept the invite to Beau's bachelor party to keep an eye on him and see if he'd fuck up on his last night as a free man. Especially because he seemed like the son of a bitch that would fuck a stripper just to show off in front of his groomsmen.

However, I was there for my best friend.

After we left what I now called hell, the party bus drove us to our final destination, a winery close to the castle.

Livvy grabbed my arm, giggling as she stepped off the bus.

"You're lucky I'm feeling generous, and I didn't pull your ass off that stage."

"Aw, come on! Did you see the moves on that guy? That was the real-life Magic Mike. Actually, that man would have given Magic Mike a run for his money."

"I wasn't paying any attention to him. My eyes were on you and how much you loved it."

"I mean... what's not to love? The confidence alone was a turn-on."

"That's what gets you going these days?"

She chuckled, walking into the private room they set aside for us.

"I'll never tell." She wiggled her eyebrows.

After the attendant checked us off the reservation list, she introduced us to our hostess, and for the next hour, we drank entirely too much wine.

An hour later, we sat at the bar, doing our taste testing. When she started giggling uncontrollably over nothing, I knew the drinks were starting to get to her. Livvy was such a lightweight

She pointed at the empty glass. "That one is my favorite." She smiled, eyes a little hazy and cheeks a bit flushed.

She really is beautiful.

Reaching over with the same expression, she grabbed my drink.

"Are you planning on stealing my wine for the rest of the night?"

"Only the ones that taste like fruit. Look." She scooted the drier wine to me. "I'll switch with you. You drink those, and I'll drink these. Boom! We're even."

"Boom, huh?"

"Yep."

"I think you might need to slow down."

She nodded to the darker glass of wine. "That one tastes like shit."

"How do you know? You're making me drink it."

"I know because I can read." She narrowed her eyes at the label. "At least I think I can. What time is it?"

I looked down at my watch. "Almost eleven."

"Mmmm kay." Leaning into me, she rubbed her nose against my neck. "You smell good... do you always smell this good?"

I scoffed out a chuckle.

"Why haven't I noticed how good you smell?"

"You're not usually making out with my neck."

"I've made out with your neck before and your face."

I grinned. "My face?"

"Yeah." She touched my mouth. "Like here. I've made out with those."

"I think I need to get you some food."

"I've also made out with your dick. You really loved it when I did this thing with my tongue. It always made you do this deep growl, like, roar!"

"On that note." I grabbed the drink out of her hand.

"Hey... why are you taking that away from me? I wasn't done."

I stood, taking her with me before nodding to the women. They must have noticed Livvy wobbling since they smiled and nodded back in understanding that I was getting her out of there. Once we arrived at the castle, I made her drink a glass of water and take three pain relievers. She ate a bit of food but was adamant that she wasn't drunk and didn't need it.

There wasn't a cloud in the sky as we stood on her terrace that overlooked the gardens of the estate. The gentle lull of the breeze and honey scent was running heavy through me. She leaned her head on my shoulder, and I tried not to think about the fact that this would be the last time we'd be together for who knew how long.

The mere thought brought a sudden sadness over me.

Can I do this? Can I really let her get married to a man who isn't me?

"What are you thinking about over there?" she questioned, tearing me away from my thoughts.

I didn't hesitate in rasping, "Tomorrow."

LIVVY

"Yeah, I've been thinking about tomorrow a lot today too."

I swallowed hard, hearing him admit what I already knew. Ethan and I always shared a connection I could never explain or understand. This unspoken bond, where words weren't needed to know how we were feeling.

He was my person.

I was his.

My mind ran rampant with question after question I'd been thinking about all week. Aware of what I needed at that moment, he placed his arm around my body, pulling me into the nook of his arm. I felt him inhale a deep, steady breath as he hugged me closer to him, kissing the top of my head.

We stayed like that in complete silence, watching the world revolve around us like we were the only two people in it.

"You ready?"

Giving in to the emotions I couldn't seem to control, I snapped, "What a loaded question, Ethan. If you're asking me if I'm ready to go to bed, I'm fine. Now, if you're asking me if I'm ready to get married tomorrow, then my response would be, I'm not so sure anymore. Is that normal? To second-guess?"

"You sound upset."

"I'm not. I'm just asking my best friend."

Sweeping the hair away from my face, he placed it behind my ear. "I can't answer that for you."

"Why not?"

"It's not my place, Livvy."

"Then whose place is it?"

"Only yours."

"It's going to change everything."

"It won't change us being best friends."

"Promise?"

"What are you so worried about? I'm not the one getting married."

Am I making the right choice? Could I do this? Do I still want to? What am I trying to prove? What am I trying to find that isn't already in front of me?

The more I thought about it, the less confident I felt that I could truly do this...

"I love Beau," I stated in a serious tone.

"I'm not the one you need to convince."

"Are you saying you think I should marry him?"

"Livvy, what do you want me to say?"

I didn't know if it was the booze, the fact I'd been drinking all night, or if it was just Ethan being there with me this entire time and my whole life. At that moment, I couldn't for the life of me picture a future with anyone but him. This was my last chance to possibly make things right. Ethan was right. This was my life, not my parents' life. I had to do what was right for me.

"I want you to tell me the truth." I peered deep into his eyes. "Do you love me?"

"Of course, I love you."

"I know you love me, Ethan. I love you too. But I need to know, are you in love with me? Do you not want me to marry Beau?" Without thinking twice about it, I confessed with tears in my eyes, "Because if you tell me not to marry him, if you tell me that you're in love with me... then I won't do it. I won't marry him tomorrow. I just need to hear you say it. Please, Ethan... tell me what to do."

He gripped my face. "Livvy, I've been in love with you since before I knew what that even meant. You have to know that."

"It's been so long... I don't know anything anymore."

"You'll always be my girl. I love you more than anything in this world. I think about that summer all the time. I think about the first time we made love and every time after. I think about the way you feel, the way you taste, the way I feel when I'm with you."

Tears slid down the sides of my face.

"I think about what would have happened if you were pregnant."

I sucked in air, hanging on by a thread.

"I think about how much I would have loved you being the mother of my child. How much I would have loved being the father of yours. I think about the future we could have had, but mostly..." He leaned forward, getting close to my lips. "I think about how I lost you. I think about how I just let you slip through my fingers. I was so busy trying to make a name for myself so that your parents would finally accept me. So that your father would shake my hand with admiration and respect, possibly calling me son like I've seen him do all week with your fiancé."

"Ethan... I had no idea."

"It's always been you, Livvy, and it will always be for me. You're my soulmate. I'll always be in love with you."

The uncontrollable tears flew endlessly.

This was the moment.

The second.

The time that Ethan and I could finally be together, and I couldn't have been more ready for it.

"I'm sorry, Ethan. I should have never said yes to Beau. Not when I've always been in love with you. Tell me not to marry him, and I swear to you I won't."

I waited.

And waited.

And waited...

Until he finally said, "I can't tell you that. As much as I want to, as much as I wish I could, I can't make that choice for you. I'd be no better than your parents. It needs to come from you, Livvy, or you'll always remember that you didn't marry him because I told you not to. I love you too much to risk the chance of you regretting your decision and blaming me for it."

He kissed away my tears, rubbing his soft lips along my heated skin that felt like it was on fire.

I felt like I was on fire, burning inside and out.

"Ethan, please..." I begged.

Instead, he kissed the corner of my mouth like he did the first night, letting his lips linger.

"I'm sorry," he cautiously spoke. "I can't."

With that, he turned around and left.

I broke down.

I bawled.

Big, huge, ugly tears.

I cried until I couldn't breathe.

Until I couldn't speak.

Until I couldn't cry anymore.

Then I got up, jumped in the shower, and went to bed. Because tomorrow, I'd become...

Mrs. Elizabeth Hunter.

Chapter Twenty-Eight

ETHAN

I barely slept that night.

I'd never forget the expression on Livvy's face as she begged me to tell her not to marry Beau. It'd be a memory that would forever haunt me. Trust me, it took everything inside me not to ask her to marry me instead.

My time was up, and I couldn't believe my team didn't find one fucking thing on her fiancé, soon-to-be husband. I couldn't have our conversation end the way it did. The ceremony was only two hours away, and after I finished getting dressed in my tux for my best friend's wedding, I had to talk to her and make things right between us.

Her door was slightly open, and it was almost like I had an out-of-body experience. Slowly, I pushed it open to reveal the most beautiful woman I'd ever seen. Livvy looked gorgeous. She stood in front of the floor-to-ceiling mirror, wearing a white lace wedding dress as she stared at herself in the reflection. I stopped dead in my tracks, captivated by her. Unable to move forward.

My chest heaved.

My breath hitched.

My body froze.

She didn't try on this dress that morning. This one was new and so fucking perfect for her.

Within seconds, we locked stares through the mirror. Our emotions poured out of us, bleeding on the ground beneath us. I shut the door, locking it behind me.

"You look gorgeous, Livvy," I breathed out, suddenly standing close behind her.

"Thank you," she replied in a gentle tone. "You don't look so bad yourself."

I shook my head and asked, "How did we get here?"

"I don't know. I wish I knew, but we're here, nonetheless. At least I know where you stand now, Ethan."

"That's not fair."

"How else am I supposed to feel?" She pointed at herself. "I basically throw myself at you, and you—"

"You think that was easy for me? You think I want you to marry him! You're literally marrying the first man who paid attention to you!"

"Bullshit! If that were true, then I'd be marrying you!"

She immediately turned to face me. "I love him!"

"No, you love the idea of him. You love that it's comfortable. You love that your parents approve of him! You love that it's easy! You love that you think this is what you're supposed to be doing. You're trying to make everyone else happy, even if you're miserable. You've always been this way, but when will you start putting what you want first? When will that matter? Because you're running out of time, and I can't just stand back and let you marry the wrong man!"

"You're doing this now? You're doing this to me hours before my wedding? I asked you last night. No, I begged you last night—"

"I can't do it for you! What part of that do you not understand?"

Her chest rose and fell with each word that fell from my lips.

"Let me touch you, Livvy. Let me prove to you that everything I say is true."

Our faces were inches apart, and I felt her everywhere.

Her body.

Her soul.

Her heart.

It was right there for me to remind her who she belonged to. Who she'd always belong to.

"Tell me to leave, Livvy. Tell me to go. Tell me that you don't wish it were me that you went to bed with every night and woke up to every morning. Tell me you want this, and I swear I'll leave it alone. I'll watch you marry Beau and not say a damn word. Just let me hear you say it to me."

"Ethan," she warned in a tone I didn't recognize.

I set my forehead on hers, gripping her face between my hands.

She shut her eyes.

She had to.

She knew I could see right through her.

"Ethan," she panted, her breathing mimicking mine. "Please..."

"Please what, Livvy?" I rasped, hanging on by a thread. "Huh? Please what, baby?"

"You're right..." She opened her eyes, staring straight into mine. "I can't do it. I can't marry Beau. Not when I've always been in love with you." She frantically shook her head. "Oh my God, Ethan... what am I doing?"

"It's okay," I coaxed, instantly relieved. "It's going to be okay."

"I have to tell him," she stressed. "I have to tell him right now."

"Livvy, you need to—"

Before I could say anything more, she hauled ass out of the room, and what happened next...

I never expected in a million years.

Not for one second.

LIVVY

What the hell was I doing? How did I not see I'm making a huge mistake until now? What is wrong with me?

Livvy!" Ethan shouted behind me as I ran through the castle wearing my wedding gown, heels, and veil.

I was decked out and ready to go. My makeup was done, and my hair was finished. I'd spent four hours in that glam chair just aimlessly gazing out the window, lost in my thoughts. My life played out in front of me as if it were nothing more than a movie reel I watched in the theater.

After last night, I realized how confused I truly was and how much I wanted to make everyone else happy. I spent my entire life doing what my parents wanted, and through the years, it felt like piece by piece of me was being chipped away little by little. I couldn't believe I let it get this far.

I did love Beau, and I hated that I'd be hurting him, but I'd hurt him even more if I said, "I do." This wasn't fair to him. He deserved to be with a woman who was head over heels in love with him.

"Livvy!" Ethan hollered.

From an outsider looking in, I must have been quite the sight. The bride running as fast as she could in six-inch stilettos with her man of honor chasing her.

Once I tore through the door of his suite, Beau snapped around, cocking his head to the side with wide eyes. He was getting dressed.

"Isn't it bad luck to see the bride before the wedding?"

"We need to talk."

"Words every man wants to hear."

"Livvy!" Ethan ran in after me, and Beau's gaze shifted from me to him.

"What's going on?"

For some reason, I couldn't help but notice the expression of pure panic on Beau's face. It was quick, but I saw it.

"Is everything alright?" he questioned.

"Ethan." I turned to face him. "I need to speak to Beau alone."

He eyed me skeptically for a few seconds before he nodded. "I'll be right outside."

"Why does he need to be right outside?" Beau asked as Ethan shut the door behind him. "What's going on, Elizabeth?"

"Beau…" I whispered in a tone I didn't recognize. "Why do you want to marry me?" I finally asked, needing to know.

His eyebrows pinched together. "What kind of question is that?"

"It's a question I need you to answer."

"It's a stupid question."

"Why can't you answer it?"

"Because I love you."

"I know that."

"Then why are you asking?" She shook her head. "What is this? Some kind of test? Isn't it a little late for this, sweetheart?"

"It's a simple question, don't you think?"

"I gave you my answer. I love you, that's it. There's no mystery you have to solve here. I want to marry you because I love you."

"Alright... then why do you love me?"

"You're starting to scare me."

"Beau, please just answer. Why do you love me?"

He rubbed his forehead. "I'm trying really hard to stay calm, Elizabeth, but you're making that very difficult."

"What kind of life do you see us having?"

"A happy one," he uttered in one breath.

"And if I don't want to move? If I don't want kids? That's okay with you?"

"We're back to this again?"

I'm going to ask this one last time, and please, please, just be honest with me. Why do you want to marry me, Beau?"

"I've waited so long for you. I mean, you know that. You're mine now."

"So I'm a trophy?" I murmured loud enough for him to hear.

"I didn't say that."

I shrugged, backing away.

"You didn't have to."

Chapter Twenty-Nine
LIVVY

"Elizabeth, why are you making problems?"

"Does it have anything to do with the fact that I'm a Collins? Would you be marrying me if I wasn't?"

"Elizabeth…"

"Your silence is deafening, Beau."

"I'm not silent. You want me to lie and tell you I don't like the fact that you're a Collins? Of course, I like it. I'm a Hunter; you're a Collins. Sweetheart, we just make sense. I love you. We're together now. I want to move on with our lives. I want to get married. I want to have kids. I want—"

"What about what I want?"

"Isn't that what you want?"

"No, you've never asked me. Nobody's ever asked me except for Ethan."

"So what? He gets a medal for asking you a question?"

"At least he's interested in my answer."

"It doesn't matter!" he roared, getting in my face. "I'm the one who's been here for the past ten years. I'm the one who's been fucking you, feeding you, and soon, I'll be financing you. I've always had you. I'm the one who's marrying you. You'll be my wife. Mrs. Hunter. His asking you meaningless questions doesn't change anything. You're mine.

At the end of the day, I have you, and all he has is your pitiful friendship."

I jerked back, blurting, "The wedding. I'm not marrying you, Beau."

"What?"

"You heard me. I'm sorry, but I'm not marrying you. I should have never said yes."

He reached for me. "You don't mean that."

I stepped back. "I do. I've never meant anything more in my life. You don't love me, Beau. You just love the way we look together. You love the attention that we gather. You love the idea of me. You're not in love with me. You have no loyalty to me. It's my status that you're after."

"What the fuck?" he deeply roared again, hovering above me.

At that moment, Ethan slammed the door open. I blinked, and he stood in front of me, placing me behind him.

"You want to try that again?" Ethan threatened with a menacing regard.

"Oh…" Beau nodded with a frenzied expression. "I get it now… you found out, didn't you?"

I opened my mouth to ask him what he was talking about, but Ethan held his hand out behind him, silencing me. Ethan could always read people, and it was as if he expected Beau would play right into his hands. I guess that was what made him such a great businessman. He knew how to call your bluff.

In one stride, Ethan stepped up to him. "Did you think I wouldn't find out?"

"You son of a bitch," Beau bit, fisting his hands.

Ethan didn't back down, remaining calm. Almost like a snake about to attack its prey.

"How long have you known? You must have just found out, or she would have already confronted me. How did you do it? Huh? Hire someone to watch me?"

"That's just the tip of the iceberg."

"What proof do you have?"

"All the proof I need."

Beau's panicked expression shifted back to me. "Elizabeth, let me explain."

I swallowed hard, playing along like I knew what he was going to confess.

"They mean nothing to me." He rushed over to me before the last word left his mouth. "Do you understand me? I love you."

I lifted my eyebrows.

Is he saying what I think he is?

"A man of my caliber is put in situations where it's expected of him, but, sweetheart, they're just a fuck." He grabbed my face. "I come home to you. You're the one I want to be my wife, my partner, the mother of my children. You're Mrs. Hunter."

My mouth dropped open, yanking my face away from his grasp. "You piece of shit! You've been cheating on me?"

"Elizabeth, Ethan doesn't know all the facts—"

"You're right, you fucking asshole! He doesn't know shit! You're the one who just told on yourself!"

Beau's face immediately paled. "What?"

"I can't believe you! You were going to marry me after sleeping with other women? Oh my God! While you're still sleeping with me?!"

Beau glared at Ethan. "You fucking played me?"

"Like a fiddle," he replied.

"You motherfucker!" He went for Ethan, but I jumped in front of him.

"That's what you care about? That's who you're going to fight with? I just found out you've been sleeping around behind my back, and you want to battle it out with Ethan instead of with me? You're a shameless piece of shit!" I pushed him as hard as I could. "How dare you use me?"

"Use you?! You really want to play that card? We've been using each other!"

"Screw you! I may not be in love with you, but I still love you, Beau! I respect you, while you obviously have none for me."

"Elizabeth, you need to understand. It's just the way it is. You think your father has been faithful to your mother all these years? Every man at our status fucks around. It's nothing. It's just sex. There're things I won't ask of you because I respect you, so there's that."

"Oh..." I faintly nodded. "It's my virtue you respect. How ironic.

What? Do you want me to thank you? You're unbelievable if you think that you deserve that. And just for the record." I pushed him again. "I know in my heart my father would never cheat on my mother! I don't care what sick and twisted things you've conjured up to excuse your infidelity, but if you think for one second that I'm going to accept your ridiculous excuse and actually marry you, then you're a bigger asshole than I think you are!"

"Sweetheart—"

"Don't talk to me!" I threw my hands out in front of me. "Don't even look at me! You lost the right to even be allowed to look at me!"

With that, I abruptly turned in my veil, and it flew behind me.

"Elizab—"

He rushed after me, but I didn't stop for one second. I needed to find my parents. The famous photographer was probably pissed I was late to my pre-wedding shoot around the castle. It was why I had to get ready so early.

I hated that I was possibly going to make my parents look bad.

I hated that I would look like a runaway bride.

I hated that I was mostly going to embarrass my father's name. Especially since he was eventually going to run for president.

On my way to their suite, I ran into him and my mother, frantically looking for me.

"There you are!" Mom reprimanded. "Elizabeth, we've been calling your cell phone for the past thirty minutes! You have the photographer—"

"Mom, I know! I'm so sorry!"

Dad took one look at my crazed expression and asked, "Honey, what's going on?"

I loved that despite our tough love relationship, he still knew I was going through something.

"Daddy, I'm so sorry. I'm sorry for everything, but I can't marry Beau."

Beau snapped, "The hell she isn't!" Stomping up beside me, he lied, "Sir, please excuse your daughter. She's just having cold feet. It's nothing."

"Oh, it's nothing?" I seethed, glaring at him. "You cheating on me is now reduced to nothing?"

Mom shouted, "Cheating on you?"

"Sir"—Beau nervously chuckled—"I've been trying to explain to her about men of our status and how meaningless it all is. I'm very much in love with your daughter."

I jerked back, truly amazed he honestly believed everything that came out of his mouth. This man was seriously delusional.

"Oh my goodness," Mom exclaimed, mortified. "Elizabeth, get over here!" She sternly pointed at Beau. "You should be ashamed of yourself! Our daughter is not a toy you can play with!"

"Sir..." Beau continued. "Please..."

I'd never seen Beau's face like that. He clearly expected my father to side with him. He was acting like an entitled child, throwing a tantrum because he didn't get the prize he thought he deserved.

The anger radiated off his body in waves, and his eyes were feral. It was the first time in my life I didn't recognize the man standing in front of me. The man I spent the past ten years on and off with.

This was not the Beau I knew, and everyone in the room could sense something was off with him. Before the thought could even cross my mind, it all happened so quickly.

My father didn't hesitate in spewing, "Get the fuck out of my face. You don't deserve the ground she walks on. There is nothing or anyone more important to me than my girls! Now get out of my face before I do it for you."

I slightly gasped. I'd never seen my father react like that.

"This is bullshit!" Beau tightly grabbed my arm, dragging me away. "Let's go! We're getting married now!"

"Ouch! Beau, you're hurting me! Let go!" For a moment, I struggled to break free from his grasp.

Out of nowhere, Ethan's fist was clear across Beau's nose, and he yanked my arm out of Beau's grasp. Beau dropped to the ground like a sack of potatoes.

Everyone's wide stares flew to Ethan as he shook out his right hand, only glaring daggers at Beau, who was groaning on the tile floor, holding his nose as blood gushed out.

He spat, "My nose, you fuck!"

"I've been waiting to do that since the second I laid eyes on you. That was one for me."

I warned, "Ethan—"

In one swift kick, Ethan hit Beau in his groin. "And that one's for Livvy, you piece of shit!"

I stood there in a state of shock, it finally all hitting me like a ton of bricks.

"Ethan," Dad yelled as Mrs. Hunter shrieked from across the hall.

"Get her out of here!" Dad ordered. "I'll handle everything! Just get her out of here now! Go out the back to avoid the press! I'll have my guards meet you two out there! Take her out of the country! I don't care where you take her! Just get her out of here! Keep her safe and out of the press!"

Why is my dad screaming?

It was only then I realized chaos had erupted all around me. Mrs. Hunter was on her knees, screaming for a doctor as her husband ran toward them. There were maids, butlers, and guests beginning to come in our direction.

Ethan was suddenly in my face. "We've got to go."

"Go where?"

"Anywhere but here."

"I can't just let my parents take the humiliation for all this. I have to—"

"Livvy," Dad interrupted, making me look at him.

He'd never called me that before, and I think he knew it was the only thing that'd get my attention with the disaster exploding around us.

"You'll always be my baby girl. I have this. Okay?" Dad kissed my forehead. "Go. Please go with your best friend."

He'd never called Ethan that, either.

"I'm sorry I failed you," Dad whispered in my ear before shaking Ethan's hand to express his gratitude. "Thank you."

The next thing I knew, I was on Ethan's private plane...

Still in my wedding gown, veil, and shoes.

Chapter Thirty

ETHAN

ONE MONTH LATER

"Yeah," I said to my lawyer on the phone, watching Livvy wake up from her nap on my couch.

We were in my secluded home in the Bahamas. Nobody aside from my team knew about this property. This was where I came to escape the mayhem of my world.

"How is she holding up?" he asked.

"She's doing better."

"Does she know about what her father did?"

"Not yet."

"She's in for a surprise."

"I'm as shocked as everyone else."

"Did you know before the story ran?"

"I didn't. My job was just to keep her safe and out of the press."

Her gaze fluttered open.

"She's getting up. I'll call you back." I hung up.

"Hey." Livvy groggily stirred, sitting up.

"Feel better?"

She rubbed sleep from her eyes. "I think so. I swear, every time I wake up, for a split second, it feels like the past month was just a dream."

"I know." I sat down beside her. "It'll get easier."

"I can't believe I didn't see it. How could I have been so blind to Beau cheating on me? I feel like such an idiot, and I wasted ten years of my life with a man who didn't love me when I had you the entire time. I'm never going to forgive myself for that, Ethan."

"Livvy, there is nothing to forgive. You never led me on. I've been here because I wanted to be. They were all my decisions. You never told me not to be with anyone. As a matter of fact, I'm the one who told you to promise me you were mine first… I couldn't let you go, and I never did, but it was because I wanted to. I don't blame you for anything. I hope you know that."

"I do, but that doesn't keep me from blaming myself. We lost so much time together, and now where does all of this lead us? For the past month, we've played house. You've been hiding me in your gorgeous estate on this breathtaking island as if we're on our honeymoon or something. I can't help but feel like a fool."

For the past month, Livvy and I just hung out like we used to. I tried to keep her distracted and away from the horrible things the press was saying about her until this morning. At the end of the day, we were best friends first, and it was the core of our relationship.

The rest would fall into place eventually. Especially now that we were both on the same page about our feelings for each other.

"I know, but the media is mutilating me right now. I'm literally the runaway bride."

"Yeah… about that."

Her eyebrows pinched together. "What?"

"An article for *People* magazine was released while you were sleeping."

"Oh God… did Beau do an interview? What did he say?"

"It wasn't Beau. It was your old man."

She winced. "How bad is it? What did he say?"

Until now, all Mr. Collins had done was have his lawyer release a statement asking the media to respect their privacy. The Hunters' lawyer did the same. The press were the ones creating the fake stories and gossip to sell their lies.

There were a few magazines I was able to pay off and even more reporters I was able to threaten, but I could only do so much. Publications still came out about the situation, and sadly, they pinned Livvy as the villain.

That was until this afternoon.

"What's going on?" she questioned. "You're freaking me out."

"Here." I handed her my iPad, open to her father's interview. With a jittery grip, she grabbed it.

There, in front of her eyes, she read the article where Mr. Collins took full responsibility for what happened, telling the magazine that his daughter was marrying Beau because he pressured her to do it. He went on to say that he had planned out her whole life, and it came back to bite him in the ass, hurting Livvy in the process. He then proceeded to show evidence of Beau's infidelity and how much he regretted letting this snake use his baby girl. Mr. Collins took full responsibility for what happened and the role he played, which only made the public love him more.

He was now viewed as the father protecting his little girl—like every father should. Beau was painted for the piece of shit he was, and I, for one, was enjoying every second of it.

By the time Livvy finished reading, tears streamed down her face.

"I can't believe he did that for me."

"I know."

"I don't even know what to say about it."

I pulled her into a tight hug.

LIVVY

I stayed in Ethan's arms for I don't know how long, desperately trying to find some answers in the comfort he always provided me until my cell phone rang.

"It's my dad's ringtone." I grabbed it off the coffee table. "Hey, Dad."

"Hello, honey. How are you holding up?"

He called at least once a day to check in on me, same with my mom.

"I'm better now. I read your article. Why didn't you tell me about it?"

"I didn't want you to talk me out of it. Your mother didn't know either."

"Daddy, I'm so sorry about everything. I really hope this won't affect your candidacy next term."

"If it does, so be it."

After a long pause, he said, "I'm very proud of you, Elizabeth, and I need you to know that."

"Thanks, Dad. It means a lot to me, but I also want to say what happened with Beau isn't your fault. I need you to know that too. He had us all fooled."

"That's not what makes it my fault. If it weren't for me, you wouldn't have thought you had to marry someone like him. A prestigious last name like Hunter was all I ever wanted for you. I thought that would make whoever you did marry a good man, and I forgot it doesn't matter. A last name doesn't make a good person, and I know that, but for some reason, it seemed like it was the best option for your future, and for that, I take full responsibility."

I half smiled. "I love you, Dad."

"I should have trusted your ability to make the right choices."

Ethan nodded at me, mouthing, "I have to take this call." He stood and left.

"How's Ethan?" he asked out of nowhere.

"He's good."

"He's always been good to you, huh?"

"Yeah," I said. "You know, it's not too late for you to get to know him. I know he'd like that."

"Your mom likes him. She's always liked him."

"I know," I agreed, being grateful for that.

"Maybe we could all have dinner some time."

I knew this was how he was trying to make amends.

"That would be great."

"I love you, sweetheart."

"I love you too, Daddy."

We hung up, and I immediately felt like a huge weight had been lifted off my shoulders. At least now my relationship with my father would get better, and I could get to know the man everyone loves. Ethan walked back into the room with his cell phone in his hand.

"Everything okay?"

He slipped it into his back pocket. "Just work stuff."

"You probably need to get back to Charleston?"

"Don't worry about me. How are you? How was the call with your dad?"

"It was good. He said a lot of things that I've needed to hear for a long time."

"I'm glad you could fix things between you two. I know how important they are to you."

"Me too." I stepped toward him, wrapping my arms around his neck. "I'm ready."

He grinned, pulling me closer to him. "Ready for what?"

"I'm ready for you to take me home." Speaking with conviction, I added...

"And I'm not talking about California."

Chapter Thirty-One

ETHAN

TWO MONTHS LATER

"Is this the last box?" I questioned, setting it on top of the table in Livvy's new home in Charleston.

"Yes!" She beamed. "I have officially moved into my new house. "I'm so excited!"

She looked beautiful wearing overalls, and her long, red hair was down. She leaned against the doorframe with her arms crossed over her chest.

"This is my home, Ethan. This town has always been my home. I never wanted to leave, but I'm thankful I did. It gave me the chance to realize this is where I belong."

I nodded, understanding.

"I think we need a break."

"You have been a slave driver all morning." I grinned. "What do you have in mind?"

While Livvy got her life back together and in order, I helped her however I could. She quit her job and opened up her own firm, focusing on corporate law. I was her first client—her father was her second. Things were slowly but surely falling back into place for everyone, me included.

I was happy to have my girl back in town, close to me. Despite everything that happened and what we said, we knew where the other stood. I was waiting to see where we'd take things in our friendship now that life had settled.

"It's a surprise," she replied, smirking like a fool. "Come on."

I followed her into the garage. With a happy smile, she showed me what was buried deep in one of her boxes.

"I can't believe you kept them." I chuckled, amazed that she was holding our old skateboards.

"Of course, I kept them. I have something else too."

"What?"

She reached into her pockets, pulling out my lock and key necklace. In a flirty expression, she asked, "Want to help me put it on?"

I nodded. "I'd love nothing more."

After I was done, she turned to face me again. "Thank you."

"I love seeing it where it belongs."

She beamed, holding up our boards. "You up for the challenge?"

I grabbed my board out of her grasp. "I'm not the one who was slow as shit."

"Hey! You're taller than I am. Your stride is going to go faster."

"You're still using that excuse?" I threw it on the ground, and in one swift movement, I jumped on it and effortlessly slid across her driveway.

"How are you still so good at that thing?"

"I'm good at everything."

She giggled, setting her board on the concrete before she carefully stepped onto it.

"Wimp!" I teased. "But you are just a girl."

Her mouth dropped open. "Oh! I'm going to get you, Ethan Carter."

"You'll have to catch me first."

For the next hour, we skated around her new neighborhood. We got in my truck, without either of us suggesting it, and ended up at our waterhole.

"Did you purposely buy a house near this place?"

She shrugged with a guilty expression. "I'll never tell."

"What now?" I asked, taking in the way her red hair still reflected off the sun.

I expected her to start splashing me with water, but instead, she asked, "Why do you love me, Ethan?"

"Is this a question game?"

In a serious tone, she ordered, "No more games."

"Alright, fair enough." I repeated her question. "Why do I love you?"

"Yes. Why does one of the richest men in the world love me?"

"Money means nothing to me."

"You wouldn't think that with all your estates and cars."

"Those are investments."

"Says every billionaire."

I cocked my head to the side, baiting, "You talk to a lot of billionaires, Livvy?"

She stepped back into the water, never taking her sparkling eyes away from me. "Once or twice, but you're the only one worth a damn."

My feet moved of their own accord, only stopping when I was close enough to touch her.

I didn't.

Her honey scent assaulted my senses from the light breeze in the air coming my way.

"Since the first day I met you, dressed in overalls like you are now. Your hair was in pigtails, and your freckles were prominent on your cheeks and nose. They were so enticing. I remember looking up at you from my bus seat and being mesmerized by them. I remember wanting to count them so I would know how many freckles were on your face."

"Ethan..."

"Since that moment, you've always been my favorite thing to look at. I know everything about you. The way your eyes shine bright when you're unbelievably happy. The way your smile can literally make my heart race. The way your laughter has always been so fucking contagious. I know the way you feel, the way you taste, the way you love... You were my first kiss, Livvy. You were my first everything." I paused to let my words sink in. "It doesn't matter where I go, where I'm at, or who

I'm with, it's always been you. You ask me what I love about you, Elizabeth Collins? It's more like what I don't love about you. There is no me without you." I grabbed the sides of her face, and she leaned into my embrace.

"You were mine first. You're my girl, baby."

Her mouth parted, and I glided my thumb across her bottom lip. "I'm not going to tell you it's always been easy because it hasn't, but that's never mattered between us. You understand what I'm saying?"

She nodded, looking at me all doe-eyed.

"And I'm sorry it's taken me this damn long to finally, finally do this." Tugging her toward me with my hand on the crook of her neck, I kissed her.

"I love you," she moaned in my mouth.

"I love you."

My hands gripped her ass to wrap her legs around my waist as I carried her to the bed of my truck. Once I set her down on the edge, I stood between her legs. What started off innocent turned into something else entirely. Our hands began to roam, not being able to decide where we wanted to touch each other the most.

When her small, delicate hand found my cock, she moaned again.

"Fuck," I growled into her lips as she stroked me up and down, her hand barely closing around my shaft.

I leaned back and helped her take off her top. My mouth instantly sucked on her nipple, flicking and swirling it before moving over to the other hardened peak, making her moan in pleasure. Forcefully yet gently, I played with her sensitive bud until she was at my mercy.

I kissed and licked my way down to her stomach, her body responding to every sensation inflicted by my mouth. Everywhere I touched left behind a trail of fire in its wake. The feelings lingered on each caress of her delicate skin, burning from the aftereffects.

I dropped to my knees, gazing up at her through the slits of my heavy eyes. My fingers laced into the sides of her panties and overalls, yanking them off in one quick, sudden movement. I tossed them beside her shirt while gazing up at her, admiring her beauty.

She was naked.

Warm.

Wet.

The mood turned dark for a second as I drank in her luscious body that had me weak in the knees. I looked at her everywhere except her eyes, wanting to remember every curve of her figure. Branding her with my heated stare.

Her body had matured—her breasts were fuller, heavier, and her narrow waist appeared slimmer, accentuating her curvy hips and slender thighs. My eyes continued to wander until they fell upon where I wanted to look the most—her pussy.

My fingers slowly spread her lips, noticing she was slick and pink and perfect.

"I can still taste your sweet little pussy in my mouth."

I took my time, kissing my way up her inner thigh, savoring the feel of her silky skin against my lips. Tightly gripping her hips, I pulled her core to the edge of my trunk and slid my tongue deep into her pussy.

"Ethan..." she purred my name, fisting my hair, using the other to support her weight.

I glided my tongue up to her clit and sucked it into my hungry mouth, giving her pussy a soft lick before I peered up at her again with a greedy glare.

"Are you going to come in my mouth?"

"Yes..."

Her eyes closed, and her head fell back, grinding her hips in a back-and-forth motion against my lips and tongue. I started off slow, moving my head from side to side and then up and down. Her hand tightly clutched onto my hair again, almost like she was trying to rip it out.

Her eyes found mine when I finally slid two fingers into her welcoming heat.

Getting her nice and ready for me.

"Oh God, Ethan..."

"You like that? Where, baby? Right here?" I hit her G-spot, causing her eyes to roll to the back of her head. "Or..." I pulled my fingers out, instantly earning a whimper from her throat at the loss of my touch. Swiftly moving my middle finger down to her ass, I growled, "You always loved this too."

She relaxed, allowing my finger to slowly glide into her tight, puckered hole. The wetness from her pussy made it easier to do so. Aiming my finger directly toward her lower abdomen, I taunted…

"Or here?"

Chapter Thirty-Two

ETHAN

"Oh God..."

I watched her unraveling from the inside out with juices dripping out of her core, possessing every part of me. With my free hand, I thrusted two fingers back into her soaking wet cunt. Simultaneously hitting her G-spot while fingering both of her holes, I returned my mouth to her clit.

Something about claiming her this way always did things to me. She trusted me with her body, and I loved that.

"Did Beau touch you here, Livvy?" I asked, referring to her pucker.

"No..."

That was all I had to hear to pick up the pace, only fueling my desire to make her come.

"Whose pussy is this, Livvy? Whose ass is this? Whose body is this? Tell me."

She moaned in response.

"Who have you always belonged to?" I sucked her clit with more determination while thrusting my fingers harder and faster.

She soaked the palm of my hand.

Drenching my chin and neck.

Causing her to lose her mind.

Shaking.

Surrendering.

She screamed in ecstasy, "You. You're the only man I've never used a condom with."

I grinned with her clit in my mouth, and hummed, "That's my girl."

Seconds later, she came hard, panting, "Ethan…"

Flicking my tongue one last time on her clit, I let her ride out her orgasm on my face until her body went lax above me with her legs loosely hanging from my shoulders and her hands falling to her sides.

Through hooded eyes, she watched as I stood between her legs like I was before.

Placing my muscular frame on top of hers.

"You make my cock so hard when you come all over my face."

Placing my dick at her entrance, I slowly slid in and out of her, taking my time. I wanted this moment to last as long as possible. Once I was deep inside, I stopped, needing to feel every inch of her pussy wrapped around my cock.

My memories didn't compare to this.

Nothing and no one did.

This was not what I imagined our first time would be like. I couldn't help but love the fact that nothing had changed between us. As if we had been doing it for years, our connection, our bond, and our love was still there, breathing this new life into us.

I could feel her pleasure on the tip of my cock, clamping on tighter and tighter with each push and pull.

With each moan that escaped her lips.

With each deep thrust of my dick.

With each clench of her pussy, stirring down to my balls.

She came…

And came…

And just kept coming.

Our hearts pounded, our skin covered in sweat, and our lungs completely out of breath. Making love right there where it all began. Completely oblivious to everything around us. Lost in our abandonment.

In our own world.

At our waterhole.

I tugged her toward me, making her sit up before I turned us so that she was now riding me as I sat in the spot she was in.

"Ride my cock, Livvy."

She didn't have to be told twice.

"Yes..." she purred, breathless.

She slowly rocked her hips until she got used to the feeling of my shaft deep inside her from a different angle. Placing her hands on my chest for more leverage, she bounced up and down.

I took her nipple into my mouth, kneading her other breast, unable to get enough of her. Her head rolled back with another moan escaping deep from her throat.

I moved one of my hands to her clit, causing her breathing to escalate as soon as she realized what I was about to do. Encouraging me, she bucked her hips forward.

"Yeah, baby. Take my cock. Just like that... Fuck me, Livvy."

I could feel her pussy tighten, gripping my cock like a vise. I grabbed the back of her neck, wanting to bring her closer, needing her body to cover mine. Our lips moved on their own, no longer having any control over our actions.

I kissed her jawline, to her neck, and deliberately made my way back to her lips. Her delicate hands moved down my chest, wanting to feel my skin against her fingertips.

"You feel so good," I groaned, thrusting my hips upward.

I roughly gripped her hips once again, moving her harder, faster, for her pleasure and mine. My pace increased as I made her ride me as hard as she could, unable to get enough of her pussy.

Our mouths parted, breathless, riding the high, waiting to fall over the edge together. I slid my tongue into her mouth when I felt her pussy throb against my dick, pulsating long and hard as I muffled her screams.

Her quivering was my undoing.

Another groan escaped from deep within my chest as I came just as hard. I leaned my forehead on hers, and I didn't even have to tell her to open her eyes to look at me. They were already open, looking lively and thriving and full of love for me.

Our mouths were parted, still touching and panting profusely, trying to feel every emotion and sensation from our bodies being one. I swear the pounding of our hearts echoed off the water, off the trees.

"I love you, I love you, I love you," she expressed, kissing me.

"Ethan..."

"Yeah, baby," I groaned between kissing her.

"You just came inside me."

"Yeah."

"We didn't use a condom."

"I know."

"And you didn't pull out."

"My come is made to be inside you."

"Well... I haven't been on birth control since Beau."

I smiled wide. "I know. I'm done wasting time. We've already done enough of that. We have known each other all our lives."

She smiled back before I asked her same question, "Why do you love me?"

We were both still trying to catch our breaths.

Our thoughts.

Until she simply responded, "Because you shared your seat with me on the bus, because you always put my needs before yours, because of the way you make me feel, the way you make me laugh, the way you have always been there for me. I love you because I don't know how not to love you. You're my soulmate, my best friend, my lover, and..." She kissed me. "I can't wait for you to be my husband one day and the father of my kids."

And just like that, I didn't hesitate for one second in replying...

"Marry me, Livvy."

Chapter Thirty-Three
LIVVY

SIX MONTHS LATER

"Mom, I want ladybugs in the flower arrangements."

She nodded, writing them down. "Why ladybugs?"

"They're for good luck."

"I love that."

Ethan came up behind me, kissing the back of my neck. We were sitting at their dining room table, planning more details for our wedding in the fall. This time around, I helped with all the details and was involved in every last step. I didn't want to miss a second of it.

We had a wedding planner, and we were getting married at our waterhole. I don't know how my mom made it happen, but she and our team were giving us the ceremony and reception of our dreams.

"You having fun?" he asked, nuzzling my neck.

"Are you?" I mocked, squirming under his touch.

"Okay, you two. Save it for after the wedding."

We wanted to do things the right way. I was still living at the house I bought, and Ethan was at his estate. Although we spent most nights together, we'd have our own places until after we were married. I was moving into Ethan's property. He was letting me redecorate to make it my own. He didn't care what I did as long as it made me happy—his words, not mine.

I planned to rent out my house instead of selling it, wanting to have an investment. Ethan constantly said that his money was mine, and I knew he meant it, but a huge part of me still wanted to have my independence. I didn't want to rely on my husband or my parents, and he respected my decision.

"Your father is trying to convince me to develop another app."

"So you guys are bonding?"

He chuckled. "Something like that."

Over the past few months, we spent a lot of time at my parents' home, the house I grew up in. I think for both of us, it would always feel like our home too. We both grew up here. Ethan and my father were getting to know one another, and it was an amazing sight to see. I loved seeing them grow closer with each passing day.

Later that night, we were in my old bedroom. My parents kept it looking the same for me, always telling me this would forever be my place too.

"Ethan, you need to stop," I chastised as Ethan lay on top of me on my bed.

"But you used to like it when we messed around in your room. Do you need me to climb through the window to remind you?"

I laughed. "I'd love to see you try to climb that tree. It's not so easy anymore. You're not a teenage boy."

"No, baby, I'm all man."

"That you are."

I kissed him deeply.

"This isn't going to get me to stop."

"What if my daddy walked in?"

"I'd show him the diamond on your finger and remind him you're bought and paid for now."

My mouth dropped open. "Ethan!"

"What? You're my property now."

"You're shameless. We can't have sex right now."

"I'll be fast."

"You're never fast."

He grinned. "I thought that was a good thing."

"It's a great thing." I smirked. "But not when my parents are downstairs."

"We've had sex with your parents downstairs before."

"Yeah, but that was different. We didn't have two houses we could screw in."

"Is that what we're doing? Screwing? I thought we were trying to make a baby."

"Ethan, bite your tongue. If my mom hears you, she'll kill me."

"You're not going to tell them, then?"

"Absolutely not."

"What if we get pregnant?"

"I'll tell them it's a miracle. My mom would murder me if she knew I might be pregnant in Vera Wang. Besides, we're not supposed to be actively trying. You're supposed to be pulling out."

"I always forget that part."

"Yeah, I'm sure."

"What?" he scoffed. "Blame your tight, wet pussy."

"Ethan!"

He pecked my lips. "I can't wait to see you in your dress."

"You've seen me in plenty."

"Those weren't for me."

I sincerely expressed, "They were always for you."

He wiggled his eyebrows. "I want to see you in silk."

"Good to know."

"Okay, now let me in." He reached for my panties.

"I let you in this morning. You still have that eighteen-year-old stamina."

"Stop being sassy."

"But you like it when I'm sassy."

I smiled, rubbing my mouth against his. "My dad is going to kill us if we don't go downstairs soon."

"Your dad and I have an understanding."

"What's that?"

I wasn't surprised when he announced, "You're mine now, and he wouldn't have it any other way."

ETHAN

Livvy was with her mom in the kitchen while I sat with her father in the living room.

"I never got to thank you for loving my baby girl the way you do."

"I don't need to be thanked for that."

"If I could go back, to this spot on the couch actually, I would have never asked you to let Livvy go."

"I know, sir."

"You've always been good enough for her. I'm sorry for how I treated you, Ethan. You never deserved it."

"You just wanted what was best for her."

"You've always been what's best for her, and I hate that it took me so long to see it." He paused for a moment. "Livvy tells me you don't have anyone but your uncle in your life."

I shook my head. "My mom died of cancer when I was a baby, and my father is... well, he's... to put it bluntly, a piece of shit."

"You close to your uncle?"

"As close as you can be with the man who raised you."

I couldn't believe how much her old man had changed in what felt like overnight. Our relationship was better than I ever thought it could be. The man looked at me with admiration. He regarded me the same way he peered at his colleagues and friends at the country club.

"You know, sir, you're a big reason I'm as successful as I am."

He narrowed his stare.

"I wanted to prove to you that I could be good enough for your daughter. You see, sir. I've always been in love with her, and I knew you wouldn't accept me unless I was on your same caliber, so I did everything I could to make sure I would be."

"Ethan, I—"

"I understand. I didn't then, but I do now. I'd want the same thing for my baby girl. Especially some boy who didn't have a family with your status. I made myself a promise that I'd be that man someday. I don't think I would have been as ambitious if it weren't for you, so in reality, thank you for pushing me to be the best man I could be. Almost like a father would."

He stood, gripping my shoulder. "It's an honor, son."

That was the first time he'd ever called me that, and I immediately remembered how much I used to hope he'd call me that one day. It was crazy to see how we'd all come full circle.

As much as I prayed for this day to eventually come, through the years I lost hope that it might come to fruition. I loved Livvy with everything inside me.

Always had.

Always would.

For the first time in my life, I had everything I wanted.

And it started and ended with...

Elizabeth Collins.

Forever mine first.

Epilogue
LIVVY

SIX MONTHS LATER

"Do you, Elizabeth Collins, take Ethan to be your husband, to have and to hold, for better or for worse, for richer, for poorer, in sickness and in health, to love and to cherish, from this day forward until death do you part?"

Looking deep into Ethan's eyes, I stated, "I do."

The minister shifted his gaze to Ethan. "Now do you, Ethan Carter, take Elizabeth, your Livvy, to have and to hold, for better or for worse, for richer, for poorer, in sickness and in health, to love and to cherish, from this day forward until death do you part?"

"I do," he murmured with fresh tears falling down my cheeks.

"Then with the power vested in me by the State of South Carolina I now pronounce you husband and wife."

Before he could say *you may kiss the bride*, Ethan couldn't restrain himself any longer. He gripped the sides of my face and tugged me to him, kissing me as if we weren't standing in front of our family and friends. Our lips crashed together in a rhythmic movement as I returned the push and pull of his mouth.

"You're mine now," he breathed out against my lips.

"I've always been yours," I promised, kissing him one last time.

The day had finally come.
Through all the ups and downs.
All the regrets.
The mistakes.
The tears.
The I'm sorry's.
The I love you's.
For every you're my girl.
And every smile and laugh.
Through the good and the bad.

It was all worth it because it got us to this point. Where nothing else mattered but being together. Ethan Carter was my first kiss, my first love, the first man who ever touched my body, heart, and soul. I couldn't have been luckier to be marrying my best friend.

Twenty-three years of friendship.
Two decades of love and devotion.
The past was behind us.
Our story was only beginning.
I was now…
Mrs. Elizabeth Carter.
The way it was always meant to be.

ETHAN

They were lucky I didn't take her right then and there in our special place no one knew about until this day. I would claim every last inch of her, from her heart to her pussy. She was mine now.

I kissed her long and deep, finally feeling at peace.

She caressed the side of my face, and I almost fell on my ass when she leaned into my ear and whispered for only me to hear…

"I'm pregnant."

Coming Soon

To find out what's next from Monica, please visit her website at authormrobinson.com

Also by M. Robinson

BECKHAM DYNASTY

Tempting Enemy

Perfect Enemy

Sinful Enemy

SECOND CHANCE SERIES

Second Chance Contract

Second Chance Vow

Second Chance Scandal

Second Chance Love

Second Chance Rival

Second Chance Mine

ANGSTY ROM-COM

The Kiss

The Fling

MAFIA/ORGANIZED CRIME ROMANCE

El Diablo

El Santo

El Pecador

Sinful Arrangement

Mafia Casanova: Co-written with Rachel Van Dyken

Falling for the Villain: Co-written with Rachel Van Dyken

SMALL TOWN ROMANCE

Complicate Me

Forbid Me

Undo Me

Crave Me

SINGLE DAD/NANNY ROMANCE

Choosing Us

Choosing You

ENEMIES TO LOVERS ROMANCE

Hated You Then

Love You Now

MC ROMANCE

Road to Nowhere

Ends Here

MMA FIGHTER ROMANCE

Lost Boy

ROCK STAR ROMANCE

From the First Verse

'Til the Last Lyric

BUNDLES

Road to Nowhere/Ends Here

Jameson Brothers

Sinner/Saint Duet

Pierced Hearts Duet

Love Hurts Duet

Life of Debauchery Duet

Good Ol' Boys

Los Diablos

EROTIC ROMANCE

VIP

The Madam

MVP

Two Sides

Tempting Bad

Meet M. Robinson

M. Robinson is the Wall Street Journal and USA Today Bestselling author of more than thirty novels in Contemporary Romance and Romantic Suspense. Crowned the "Queen of Angst" by her loyal readers, you'll feel the cut of her pen slicing through your heart as your soul bleeds upon the words of her stories with each turn of the page. Most notably known for the Good Ol' Boys, M's newest venture has graced her with the #1 Bestseller on Apple Books with Second Chance Contract. The Second Chance Men are powerful, intelligent and will sweep you off your feet and leave you weak in the knees–every woman's wildest dreams.

M. lives the boat life along the Gulf Coast of Florida with her two puppies and real life book boyfriend, the inspiration for all her filthy talking alphas, Bossman.

When she isn't in the cave writing her next epic love story, you can usually spot her mad-dashing through Target or in the drive-thru of Starbucks, refueling. Yes, she's a self-proclaimed shopaholic, but only if she's spending Bossman's money.

You can follow M, Ted, Marley, and Bossman on Facebook, Instagram, and her absolute favorite social platform–TikTok.

Acknowledgments

Personal Assistant: Renee Mccleary
Cover Designer: Pan Thao
Paperback Formatter: Swoonworthy Designs
Ebook Formatter: Swoonworthy Designs
Publicist: Danielle Sanchez
Agent: Stephanie DeLamater Phillips

Bloggers/Bookstagrammers: Without you I'd be nothing. Thank you for all your support always.

My VIPS/Readers

Street Team Leaders: Leeann Van Rensburg & Jamie Guellar
Teasers & Promo: Shereads.pang

My VIP Reader Group Admins:
Lily Garcia, Leeann Van Rensburg, Jennifer Pon, Jessica Laws, Louisa Brandenburger

Street Team & Hype Girls: You're the best.

My alphas & betas:
Thank you for helping me bring this book to life.

Made in the USA
Columbia, SC
28 February 2025